Catchman

I was reaching the edge of the cemetery when I saw something move ahead of me. Instinctively, I dropped into a crouch behind the trunk of an elm, but a moment later I was peeping round again, wanting to see who it was.

The moon eased itself out from behind the clouds, and its silver glow brightened. And just for a moment, I thought I saw – I don't know. It looked like it was hooded or something. A great big cowl, like monks used to wear, right over its face.

But in my eagerness to see it, I'd poked my head out of cover a little too much. Suddenly, the blank darkness of the figure's face snapped round and riveted me with a stare, pinning me where I was. My breath caught in my throat…

Other titles by Chris Wooding:

Catchman

Chris Wooding

Point

Scholastic Children's Books,
Commonwealth House, 1–19 New Oxford Street,
London, WC1A 1NU, UK
A division of Scholastic Ltd
London – New York – Toronto – Sydney – Auckland
Mexico City – New Delhi – Hong Kong

First published in the UK by Scholastic Ltd, 1998
This edition published by Scholastic Ltd, 2004

Lyrics taken from "Daylight Savings" are reproduced
by kind permission of Gameface

This book is dedicated to the memory of every actor or actress who bit the big one during the B-grade horror flick boom of the Eighties.
They died so we could live.

"It's gonna get dark tonight
No one wants to stay outside
No one wants to hang around
And watch the sun go down
I know you have to be home
Before the streetlights come on
I hope this one's not broken
I can nearly see my house
'Cause I can nearly see my house"

Gameface, "Daylight Savings"

I was pressed up against the hard stone wall of the Cocked Hat pub, breathing carefully and silently through the tiniest gap in my lips. Not one metre away from me, one of the Abbey Cross boys was scratching the nape of his neck. I had crushed myself into a tiny alcove, where a gutter ran from the roof down to ground level. It was dark, but there were streetlights, throwing their flat ochre glow across the tarmac of the pub's car park. I was so exposed, I couldn't believe he hadn't noticed me by now. *Duh! How dumb?*

Come on, turn around, I was thinking, trying to project my thoughts into his brain. My head began to hurt with the effort. I just needed an excuse to lamp him and I'd be away. Forget Benjy's little vendetta; I wanted some action.

I held myself back, though. This was Benjy's show, and I'd agreed not to spoil it unless it couldn't be helped. Besides, if I started on this guy, the whole of Abbey Cross would be down on our heads in a matter of minutes. Two of us against all of them. Uh-uh; *don't* think so.

The guy looked around, scanning the street either way. It wasn't more than a cursory scan; he obviously wasn't making the effort. A moment later, he was gone, never realizing that I'd been less than an arm's length away from him, hiding in the shadows.

I waited, counting seconds, listening to my heartbeat slow.

Benjy popped out of nowhere after about a minute. I hadn't seen where he'd been hiding, but I reckoned it was a place slightly more ingenious than mine. I'd been pushed for time, though. I hadn't had more than a couple of seconds to duck into that little alcove before the guy had rounded the corner.

"That was a stupid place to hide, know what I mean?" Benjy said, scowling. "You could've messed it all up."

"He didn't see me, did he? Quit moaning," I replied.

He was a broad-faced guy, stocky and wide-shouldered, wearing a black leather jacket and a battered old Paradise Lost T-shirt. If our mob – the Park Estate crew – could be said to have a leader, it was him. His abundant facial hair was the envy of most of the guys in our gang, even though he had a good couple of years on most of us. His cheeks were always thick with stubble. I wasn't quite so envious of his huge nose, or his shoulder-length brown hair, or even his questionable taste in music, but what did I know? I mean, who was going out with Leanne, anyway? Him or me? I swallowed bitterly at the thought.

He turned away from me, a little snort of disgust escaping him. He wouldn't bother arguing it any more, and that was fine with me.

2

We ran around the side of the pub and over to the back of the green. In spite of being such a dump of an estate, Abbey Cross had a pretty good-sized set of playing fields, adventure playgrounds and so on. Lot of open space. Not a good thing – dangerous. But that was half the fun.

The moon was well up as we went pegging across the grass. A few lights were on in the surrounding houses, and we glanced up at them warily.

"Over the road!" Benjy said suddenly, and he changed course. I followed him automatically, looking around for the danger he had seen. There: a group of three girls, coming around the corner of the darkened chippy. We scooted across the streetlight-soaked road and on to the small grassy area on the other side, slipping into cover behind a metal bench.

We watched the girls. Their high, shrill laughter drifted over to us through the still night. Benjy made some lewd comment, and I frowned and gently reminded him that he *had* a girlfriend. I probably wouldn't have been so boringly moral about it if his girlfriend had been anyone other than the girl *I* wanted.

Not far away was the old stone monument that the Abbey Cross estate was named after: a great big tomb in the middle of the cemetery. And towering over it, an enormous Saxon cross marking the grave of . . . I dunno, some important guy who was dead.

The heart of the Abbey Cross empire. And we were

gonna tag it. The insignia of the Park Estate guys, spray-painted right over that cross in indelible white. Benjy had his cans in his backpack; mine was stuffed in my pocket. They were *never* gonna forget tonight.

We let the ditzes walk across the park and go on their way before we emerged from cover. They probably didn't pose any threat, but both of us knew that it was best not to be seen. They'd know soon enough that we'd been here.

"Alright," Benjy hissed as we ran. "I reckon we head through Hill Street up to the cemetery. Miss out the main road altogether."

"Hill Street's gonna have more people around," I replied. "More chance of getting caught."

"The main road's too open," Benjy replied, asserting his authority. "We're going through Hill Street."

"'Kay," I said, with a mental sigh. He *would* have to do things his way. Still, it didn't really make much odds to me; like I said, this was Benjy's idea. I was just along for the ride. I didn't have anything better to do.

Hill Street was a long row of terraced houses that ran past the side entrance of the cemetery. Well, I say side entrance, but what I'm talking about wasn't much more than a couple of bent iron bars in the fence. Anyway, we crossed the green and got back on to the pavement, heading through the quiet streets. It was

4

still too bright for my liking, under the glow from the lamp-posts, but there wasn't a whole lot we could do. We had to trust to luck and hope we wouldn't get seen.

On to Hill Street, and I could tell already that Benjy had made a bad call. He knew it as well, but he was too full of himself to admit it. A good few living-room lights were still on. We could hear the mumble of conversation from somewhere nearby. From the distance came the rhythmic squeak of a kiddie roundabout, and a girl laughing dizzily. And even though we couldn't see anyone on the street, we knew that they were around somewhere.

"Let's go back around," I said. "Main road's gotta be better than this."

"What you talking about? There's nobody *there*," Benjy said, gesturing with one hammy hand.

"You can *hear* 'em," I said. "And if they see us, us it's not like they're not gonna recognize us, is it?"

Benjy knew I had a point. With his long hair and leather jacket, and my crusty dreads and manky combats, we stood out a mile in the short-haired, tracksuited world of Abbey Cross.

"We can do it. Just stay quiet."

Once again, I indicated that I didn't really care. Of course, I *would* care when fifteen of the Abbey Cross mob were trying to cave my face in with their Reeboks, but that was something I'd have to deal with when – *if* – it happened. And anyway, if it came to that, I could *run* when I needed to; a talent that's come in handy more than once before.

So we went in. We slipped along the pavement, searching for shadow whenever we could find it, but generally just hurrying onwards as fast as we could. I was really getting hyped now; we were in it deep if we got caught at this point.

The squeaking of the roundabout had stopped. For some reason, this struck me as sinister.

Coming up on our left was the cemetery, a haven of shadows.

We were there.

And then a group of guys stepped out from a jitty between two houses, a couple of girls in tow, and we were frozen there for that moment as we saw each other.

They came at us, yelling. I wasn't frozen any more.

The next few seconds were chaos. Benjy ducked into the cemetery, slipping through the bent bars, but his backpack got caught. He thrashed against it, trying to free himself. I frantically wished that he'd get his chunk butt in gear so I could get through after him, because the Abbey Cross guys were bearing down on us fast. I grabbed his pack, yanking it and shoving it through after him; he came loose, stumbling away into the darkness.

But it was too late for me to get through.

A hand grabbed my arm, but it didn't get a proper grip before I was away, darting down Hill Street. The guy who'd lunged at me crashed into the railings of the cemetery fence. The others were hollering and swearing at me.

I decided that it was probably best if I wasn't here right now, and I pegged it.

Most of them decided they were gonna come after me; a couple wormed through the fence into the cemetery and headed after Benjy. I was thrashing it down the street, my feet pounding the pavement, my dreads whipping around my face. They were close behind. I think another of them managed to get a paw to me; but like the last one, he missed with his grip and he couldn't hold on.

I bombed around the corner of Hill Street, on to Butcher Lane, skirting the perimeter of the cemetery. I don't know what I was thinking, really; maybe I was hoping to hook up again with Benjy inside, or maybe it was just that it would be easier to lose them in there. The trouble was, the cemetery was where most of the Abbey Cross guys hung out to neck beers and fag it. It was probably more dangerous in there than it was out here.

I didn't care, though. I fled along the main street, hearing my pursuers still close behind me but fading fast. One advantage about being a habitual non-smoker is that you don't start wheezing like a cat with a hairball after running fifty metres. Now I wouldn't say I was fit, but these guys were really out of shape. They couldn't hack the pace.

7

Confident with my lead, I ran up to the main gates of the cemetery, flung myself up at them and grabbed on to the top lip. A cold flake of metal bit into my hand. I ignored it, pulling myself up and deftly negotiating the spikes at the top before dropping down the other side. My pursuers ran up to the gates, making them clang loudly as they jumped up to follow me, but I was streaking into the shadows and gone.

The moon had slid behind a thick mass of cloud as I sat with my back to a gravestone, regaining my breath and picking the metal splinter out of my palm. I was still on the alert, ears honed for any sound of danger, but once they'd lost me in the darkness, I had as good as disappeared. This cemetery was big and old, with a hundred places to hide. As long as you didn't mind the company, of course: all those dead people, arranged in their little coffins. But then, I didn't really believe in ghosts.

After a while, I decided it was time to do what had to be done. Standing up, I crept silently from stone to stone, heading towards the centre of the graveyard, where the old tomb and the Saxon cross on top of it were still just visible even in the darkness. I thought I heard a rustling to my right, and went still for a moment; but when there was no other sound, I decided I'd probably been mistaken.

When I got to the tomb, there was nobody there.

I crouched behind a marble gravestone, watching and waiting. The tomb was an imposing, solid presence, a low patch of deeper darkness in the night. Somewhere, an owl with a keen sense of cliché hooted once.

This was way too easy.

Suspicious, I crossed the path that surrounded the tomb and jumped up, grabbing the top edge. The stone felt unsteady beneath my fingers, a little crumbly, but I took the risk and pulled myself up and on to the gently sloping roof. Towering above me was the cross, standing on a thick plinth. Set into the stone of the plinth was a faded brass plaque, with an inscription scored into it. It was too dark for me to read the words, and I didn't care anyway.

Glancing around one more time, unable to believe my luck, I pulled my spray-can free. The satisfying hiss of propellant gas drifted through the air as I slowly drew our insignia on to the stone: a great big stylized P, right in the middle of the cross. When the sun came up, you'd be able to see it from right across the cemetery.

I grinned to myself. Gotcha, I thought. I vaguely hoped Benjy wasn't too mad that I had to do his mission for him. But then, what if he was? It wasn't like I was all that bothered.

I scanned the graves nearby, but I couldn't see any sign of the guys who'd followed me in. I hung off the edge of the tomb, dropped to the path, and began to make my escape, weaving through the disorganized bunches of gravestones and trees, hugging the shadows. I was feeling really high, euphoric even. Abbey Cross were gonna be licking their wounds about this one for ages.

I was reaching the edge of the cemetery when I saw something move ahead of me. Instinctively, I dropped into a crouch behind the trunk of an elm, but a moment later I was peeping round again, wanting to see who it was.

I frowned. In the darkness, it was difficult to see. I thought I could just about make out a shape, like – hunched low or something, but. . .

The moon eased itself out from behind the clouds, and its silver glow brightened. And just for a moment, I thought I saw – I don't know. It looked like it was hooded or something. A great big cowl, like monks used to wear, right over its face.

But in my eagerness to see it, I'd poked my head out of cover a little too much. Suddenly, the blank darkness of the figure's face snapped around and riveted me with a stare, pinning me where I was. My breath caught in my throat. The figure stayed, unmoving, its gaze locked with mine.

I tore myself away, pulling my head back behind the elm, my back pressed up against the cold bark. Ordinarily, seeing someone in a get-up like that would have made me laugh, but right now, I didn't feel like laughing. Hesitantly, I peeped around the trunk again.

But it was gone. I stared at the spot where it had

disappeared, but I didn't catch another glimpse of the stranger. I wasn't even sure if I'd seen it at all; I've got a very potent imagination, and it's got me like that before now. But there was just something *about* that figure, though. Something that made me think – well, that it was in a whole different league to the Abbey Cross lot, if you get me.

Puzzled, and just a little disturbed, I changed course and went out of the cemetery by the other exit.

So I guess you should know who I am or something. Okay, we'll do the vital stats. My name's Davey Vale. Pretty nondescript name, all things considered, but there are a whole lot of worse alternatives, so I count myself lucky. I'm seventeen or so, about five-nine or five-ten. Around ten and a half stone, or sixty-seven kilograms for those who think the Imperial system's not good enough for them. I've got greyish-blue eyes, and this dumb nose which crooks a little 'cause I broke it getting my face filled in by this kid called Stew, who was a couple of years above me at school. Other than that, there's not too much I can tell you about my appearance. Kinda boring, really.

I dropped out of school when I was sixteen, not 'cause I was too thick but 'cause they wouldn't let me do my A-Levels if I didn't cut off my dreads. That kinda coincided with me running away from home, and between one thing and another I never really bothered picking up my education again. Never really seemed worth it to me.

So I came to the city with my mate Skeet. If you think *I'm* shiftless and lazy, you ain't seen *nothing* till you've got a load of him. Don't get me wrong, I reckon he's the best; I'm just telling you the facts. Anyway, he was going nowhere at home, so when I told him I was to leave the old dear behind and flee for greener pastures, he said (and I quote): "It's a laugh, I s'pose."

That's how much of a plan we had when we arrived here.

When I returned to Mos Eisley at about one in the morning, everybody was still up and waiting for me. Benjy rushed out as I rapped on the door, bombarding me with questions. Was I okay? Did they get me? Did I manage to pull it off? The others crowded around, but I let 'em sweat it a little before I finally raised my hands and said: "Ladeeeeez and gentlemen, the operation was a com*plete* success."

Cheers and handshakes greeted my announcement, even Benjy, though he looked a bit put out that I'd stolen his thunder. He grumbled that I'd been lucky, all the Abbey Cross guys had gone after him and chased him out of the cemetery. I kept quiet, letting him salvage his pride a little. I didn't mention that most of them had been after *me*.

We went inside then, into the living area, where a fire was burning in the grate to ward off the mild winter chill. I noticed Leanne looking at me, a smile on her face and a glint of admiration in her eyes. I returned the smile.

Mos Eisley was the name of our house. Benjy had named it after the spaceport on Tatooine in *Star Wars*. Both of us agreed that this was an excellent film, but the mook would never accept my point of view that Drew Barrymore would have been better as Princess Leia than Carrie Fisher ever could be. He had scuppered me by pointing out that Drew would have been only two years old at the time of its release, but in theory, I maintain that I'm still right.

Anyway, the place was owned by Benjy's dad. It was a property he'd inherited from Benjy's grandfather, all the mortgage paid and everything; but it was in such a rough area, and the housing market was in such a state at the time, that it wasn't worth the hassle and expense of selling. So he stripped it down to the floorboards and bare walls and sold everything inside. What was left, he said Benjy could have if he wanted.

And so Mos Eisley became the home of what was to be the Park Estate gang. At first Benjy and Leanne lived there on their own, bringing rugs for the floors and a mattress for their bed. Later, some of Benjy's friends moved into the place. And even later, me and Skeet began to crash there. We had the joke that we were pretty much the only *legal* squatters in the city. I mean, there was no water or electricity or anything, but it was free and it was a roof over our heads. And it was fun, too. Me and Skeet didn't have anything better to do.

When we were all settled, everyone demanded that I recount the story of what happened. Sitting on the rug, everyone's faces craning in close, lit by the firelight, I became the centre of attention.

I told them, of course. And of course I exaggerated and elaborated a little bit here and there, especially when I got to the bit about the figure I'd seen creeping between the gravestones. When I was finished, I looked around at everyone, awaiting a reaction.

"You really saw the Catchman?" Fiver breathed after a moment. He was a small, nervy kid. We'd nicknamed him Fiver after the rabbit in *Watership Down*. He acted pretty much the same, scared and jumpy all the time. Still, he knew a hundred ways to scam fruit machines and payphones, and as he split his gains evenly, he was the guy who kept us all afloat.

There was a silence following his suggestion. Everyone knew what he was talking about; it's not as if *I* hadn't been thinking the same thing on my way home. Over the last few months, the city had been the site of several unusual murders – stranglings, to be exact. The papers had got their teeth into it and come up with the Catchman as a twee little tag to whip up public panic. Naturally, the average sucker swallowed it without a second thought, and the Catchman had become the city's personal bogeyman.

But maybe I'm making light of this a bit too much. I mean, people *were* dying, but whether or not they were connected was a matter of opinion. And the city was frightened, no doubt about that. Girls tended not to walk alone at night any more. People glanced at

15

each other as they passed on darkened streets, each one wondering if the other was the Catchman. It was there, at the back of everyone's mind: the spectre of a killer that nobody had seen and nobody was quite sure existed . . . but it was there.

I'd always thought that the stranglings had been just coincidence, like a new fad among one of the hardcore gangs that worked the housing estates in the slum areas of the city. But after tonight, I wasn't quite so sure.

After a moment: "That's bull," Benjy said derisively.

"I never said I saw the *Catchman*," I said. "I just saw something. I dunno."

"No, but it must have been him. I bet it was," Fiver persisted, his eyes wide. "You might have been, like, right next to the most dangerous man in the city."

"Or *woman*," Leanne put in stridently. "Nobody knows who it is. It could just as easily be a woman."

Benjy sneered. "More likely it could be nothing at all. You lot are so gullible. It's just an urban myth, know what I mean? Know how many murders there are every year in a city like this?"

"Yeah, man, but how many *stranglings*?" Dino said. He was a mixed-blood Anglo–Italian. "Murder's done by knife or gun, man. Street guys and rude boys. Strangling? Too dangerous for the killer. The victim could fight back. It's the Catchman, I'm tellin' ya."

"And all the stranglings have been kids," Fiver said. "Kids our age. Never much older. That's, like, a serial

16

killer working." He glanced around at the darkness beyond the firelight.

Benjy held up his hands. "Look, you guys believe what you want. The Catchman ain't out there. Whatever Davey saw wasn't him."

"Or her," Leanne interrupted, but was universally ignored.

"And it ain't a *ghost*, either, like I've heard Win saying at least once before now."

"I never!" Win protested, colouring. She was Dino's girlfriend, a short, dumpy girl with pudgy arms who looked like she'd lived underground most of her life.

"Whatever. I'm just saying, the Catchman is some made-up guy. Just panic fire, know what I mean? People see these stranglings, and they want to put some order in it, so they make up a serial killer."

I was surprised. This was a pretty eloquent argument by Benjy's standards.

Skeet came into the conversation then. "Y'know, when you think about it, it is pretty stupid. A guy in a great big monk's habit, all done up like the Grim Reaper or somethin', he wouldn't get ten metres before someone nicked 'im."

"Look, man," Dino said. "Whatever you say, people are *dying*. And no one ever said he goes around all dressed up. No one's ever even *seen* him."

"Exactly," said Benjy. "Proves my point."

"No one ever saw Jack the Ripper either," Leanne said. "You gonna say that *he* was made-up too?"

"Thing is," Dino said, interrupting, "thing is, *something* is doing it, man. I don't know what it is, but it's real. The city's scared, man. Don't you feel that, when you go out on the streets?"

Benjy snorted. "This city never gave a toss about me ... about *us*. Let it be scared. I hope he chokes every last one of 'em. I know that nobody in the city'd care if it was us getting offed. We don't even pay taxes. We're less than nothing to those guys."

"Yeah, very revolutionary," said Leanne. "But it still doesn't explain who it was Davey saw. And if it *was* the Catchman, then Davey's the only one in the city who knows what he looks like."

"I *don't* know what he looks like," I corrected, scratching the back of my neck. "I just know that whoever it was doesn't go in for designer clothes."

"But like I said, he'd get caught if he went around like that," Skeet persisted.

"Unless he was a ghost," Win said stubbornly. She never knew when to keep her mouth shut. We spent the next five minutes making fun of her until she stormed off in a huff. Dino sighed, and raised his eyebrows at Leanne, as if to say, *see what I have to put up with*? She looked away with an expression of vague distaste, and Dino went off to go and calm Win down. There was some subtext here that I was missing, but I let it slide for now.

Benjy was looking at me triumphantly, the argument won by his side. "What?" I said. "*I* never said

I saw the Catchman. And I never said I believed in him either."

We dispersed after that. Benjy went to bed early, saying he was knackered. I was pleased that Leanne told him she would be there later; that meant she was gonna hang with me and Skeet for a while.

Leanne was Benjy's girlfriend, but she shouldn't have been. He didn't treat her right. She deserved better. I mean, Benjy's a mate and all, but not so much of a mate as I could easily forgive the way he was with Leanne. Or it could have just been that I was slightly bitter about the whole thing.

Okay, I'll be honest here. I fancied Leanne. No, not just fancied, that's not a strong enough word . . . but I'm not gonna say I *loved* her, because I don't know if I did. But anyway, let's just say that I was pretty well smitten by her. And she liked me, as well. I could tell. Even Skeet had noticed it, and he's as perceptive as a blender.

So what was the problem? I mean, *I* certainly didn't know. But in the year I'd known her, even though they'd come to the brink of splitting up so many times, she'd always stayed with Benjy. I couldn't understand it. Me and her got on so much better.

I'd stopped trying to figure it out long ago, but it didn't stop me melting like chocolate in a blast furnace whenever she favoured me with one of her smiles.

I'll give you a quick picture of Skeet and Leanne, just so you can get 'em sorted out in your head. In Leanne's case, it's obviously gonna fall way short, though. I mean, she's not a supermodel by anyone's standards, but the way I am about her – I dunno, there aren't really the words.

So, Skeet. He's kinda goofy – dumb goofy, not buck-toothed goofy – with this perpetually vacant expression on his face. Thin, like me. About the same height. His hair is all shaved down with Bic razor, basically because he couldn't be bothered maintaining a hairstyle so he figured he'd do without one. He's sorta slack-jawed and gaunt, but – well, it's like, I've known him since the world began, and his face is more familiar to me than my own. He's my mate. We're the only people dumb enough to hang around with each other.

Leanne, though. Yum. Usually I don't go for her type – shortish, strawberry blonde, wears a leather jacket like Benjy's 'cause she's a bit of a Hell's Angel wannabe – but animal attraction has no respect for class or background. She's got this rounded face, not plump but . . . umm . . . well, *rounded*, I guess. I could probably come up with a better adjective if you gave me some time but hey, do you really care that much? Anyway, her hair is blonde, like I said, and really long and straight. She's got eyes so dark they're almost black, and this really cute blunted nose that's . . . again, it's rounded. I mean, that's the best word I can think of to describe her. She's got no hard edges. Aside from making her radar-invisible, it also makes her unbearably gorgeous.

Anyway, so me and Skeet and Leanne hung around the fire, occasionally chucking bits of debris into the flames, sipping Pepsi Maxes that Fiver had bought from the local Aldi.

"Jamie and the guys are gonna be plenty mad when they wake up tomorrow," Skeet observed. He meant Jamie Archer, the unofficial leader of the Abbey Cross gang.

"I kinda think that's what Benjy wants," Leanne said. "Isn't that why you two went in there? To stir them up a bit?"

She had addressed this last question to me. I shrugged. "He didn't say as much, but I'm pretty sure he had it in the back of his mind. He's been trying to get us and Abbey Cross into a scrap for ages."

Leanne sighed. "He's never gonna let it go, is he?"

"You should know better than anyone," I replied. "This vendetta he's got is getting sorta boring."

"Yeah, I'm sick of hasslin' those guys," Skeet said. "If we weren't spendin' all our time in this dumb feud, we could have it easy. Benjy's not gonna let up till we got knives to each other's throats."

Leanne sighed again and looked morose. "He's such a stubborn idiot sometimes."

I would have agreed with her, but I thought it would be a little too obvious. I mean, I wanted them

21

to split up and all, but I didn't want her to *know* that. So I made a neutral noise. It seemed the best thing to do.

Leanne wasn't having any of it, though. "Well, don't you reckon?"

I was forced into a response. "Yeah, he's a pain like that."

There was a few moments of silence, during which the fire cracked loudly and made me jump. The others laughed at me for a bit, before Skeet said: "You know what? We should go down to Abbey Cross tomorrow, during the day. See what's up."

"You mental?" I said. "They'd kill us. 'Specially after what we've done to them."

"Nah, I mean, just stick to the main roads, keep to the outskirts, see if we can spot anythin'. It's safe enough; they ain't gonna start on us in broad daylight on a crowded street."

"That is *so* dumb, Skeet."

"Come on," he said. "We got nothing better to do."

That particular phrase was pretty much our credo, me and Skeet. Just about everything we'd done since the age of fourteen had owed its existence to that principle. Who needed reasons, anyway? We were too slack to need reasons; we just needed an absence of anything else of interest to occupy ourselves.

I was about to say no, but Leanne said: "Oh, go on, Davey. I'd love to hear about what's going on over there." She held on to my arm and gazed up at me, fluttering her eyelashes, making herself look exaggeratedly cutesy.

Well, what could I do?

"Guess so," I replied, and it was settled.

3

I'm dreaming and even though i know i am it doesn't wake me up

i'm walking through the woods except all the trees are made of rusted metal with like jagged spikes for branches and i have to be careful 'cause i know if i get scratched by one of 'em i'll get rust fever

i'm looking around 'cause i don't really wanna be here and i can see that the spiky metal trees are only one row thick all around me and past them there are fields but even though i could practically put my arm out and my hand would be out of the woods i daren't try and get out 'cause i don't wanna get rust fever whatever that is

now i can hear something nearby but i'm not sure what it is 'cause this is a dream and nothing makes much sense i just know it's a sound and so i find myself following it without really thinking about what i'm doing

so i end up in a desert and it's suddenly become really hot and i can see my dad crouched over something and he hears me and moves out the way so i can see and there's a dog there it doesn't matter what kind of dog just a dog but it's been staked to the floor on its back with each limb tied to a peg and its paws are splayed wide i think i heard somewhere that the way to handle a dog that's attacking you is to wrap your coat around your arm and hold it out in front of you and when it clamps its teeth on your arm you

24

raise your arm and drag it up then kick it under the ribs and that stops its heart

i just stand there and look at the dog which is kinda baking in the sun and it's looking at me with big stupid eyes like help me and i look at dad and he's got this big knife in his hands which gives me a bit of a shock then i turn back round and look at the dog and it's still looking at me with big stupid eyes like help me but i'm not gonna help it 'cause i don't care so i turn my back and walk away and behind me i can hear it whimper as dad goes to work on it and it doesn't make the slightest bit of difference to me

I've always been a very light and twitchy sleeper. I think it's a childhood phobia thing. This one time, I woke up with one of those great big hairy house spiders crawling on my face. You can imagine how I reacted. Anyway, since then I've always been extremely alert when I sleep. Anything much louder than a twig snapping outside wakes me up.

So it wasn't too unusual that night, when the quiet sound of the front door creaking open downstairs brought me instantly awake.

Skeet was snoring softly nearby, a dark lump on the mattress in the corner of the room. The temperature had plummeted in the pre-dawn stillness. I listened, but I couldn't hear anything else. The funny thing about my ears is that, while they might be pin-sharp when I'm asleep, they're not half so good when I'm awake. Just one of the many little quirks that makes me so lovable.

I got up, shucking off the mountain of wool blankets that I slept under, and got dressed quietly. Images were swimming through my head, pictures of the Abbey Cross mob out for revenge, sneaking into Mos Eisley to catch us unawares.

Then I thought of the figure I'd seen last night, and suddenly I felt myself go cold.

You're just making this up, I said to myself. *Stop being a kid. You're too old to be afraid of stuff like that.*

But I wasn't too old. I don't think you're ever too old. And I thought of that dark, hooded figure, gliding past the sleeping bodies downstairs like the Angel of Death, flowing like ink through the darkness. Then crouching down over its chosen victim, hunching low, long clammy fingers reaching out of its vast sleeves to wrap around the narrow throat of. . .

. . .*Leanne.*

I hurried to the door. The floor was stout and it didn't creak, but even so I was careful to keep my footsteps quiet. Slowly, I turned the handle and opened the door to the upstairs landing.

Nothing stirred. In the dim light of the cloudy winter night, the banister of the landing ran along to my right for a few metres and then turned a sharp ninety degrees, sloping downwards as it followed the staircase. I could see the bare hallway below me. Slipping out on to the landing, I looked

26

over. The front door was closed. I could see nothing below.

But what if the intruder was already inside?

I drew the butterfly knife out of my pocket, unlatched it and quietly folded it out. If it was the Abbey Cross boys, I'd make them wish they hadn't come to Mos Eisley. If it was the Catchman. . .

Don't be dumb.

I vaguely considered waking Skeet up, but discarded the idea immediately. He would be less than no use if it came to a fight. It was just that I was scared, and I wanted some company to reassure me. But if it wasn't anything, I'd just look like a mook.

I crept along the landing to the stairs, descending them step by step, pausing on each to listen and to scan the broad hallway as I went. The blank white walls were slashed with shadows. The hallway seemed too big and open, a great aching vacuum of black. I was afraid to cross it. There were at least three doors running off from it, all of them open. One led to the communal area, another led to the kitchen, and through that was Dino and Win's room. The last went along a short corridor to the downstairs bathroom (though we never used it, as the water was disconnected) and from there to Benjy and Leanne's room.

I already knew pretty much which direction I was going to take, even before I heard the dull thump, like someone bumping into something.

My heart spasmed at the sound, sending a jolt of pain through my ribs. The thump had come from the direction of Benjy and Leanne's room.

Fiver's words came back to me suddenly: *All the stranglings have been kids. Kids our age.*

My blade held out before me, I crossed the hall, my eyes fixed on the rectangle of darkness that led towards Leanne. The hair at the nape of my neck was standing up on end; I'd turned my back on two of the three doorways, and my brain was screaming danger. I fought down the sensation. Imagination. But I couldn't help a quick glance over my shoulder, brushing my dreads aside, as I padded across the too-large room.

Nothing there but shadows and silence.

I reached the doorway and peered inside. A short corridor, with two doors coming off it on the left. At the end, the window of the back door let in a distorted trapezium of dim light, spreading it across the floor. The door to Leanne and Benjy's room – the furthest one – was open.

I heard a muffled whimper from the bedroom. It was Leanne.

That was enough for me. All thoughts of personal safety gone, I sped up the corridor to her door. It stood open. My body fired with adrenalin, my knife at the ready, I stepped into the blackness.

There, against the back wall of the room, was the double-bed mattress that Leanne and Benjy slept on.

Squinting to make it out, I could see the form of Leanne, huddled under the blanket, her blonde hair spread over the pillow. She stirred again, muttering half a word, sleep-talking.

Relief flooded through me like a wave. She was okay. I watched her for a moment, in repose.

Then I heard a footstep behind me.

I whirled, the steel of my blade glinting as it spun with me, and there was a blur of movement from my attacker. An iron grip caught my wrist, and I was wrenched off my feet, thrown down hard on to my shoulder and pinned against the floor. I yelled in pain at the impact, thrashing under the weight of. . .

. . .Benjy?

"Hey! *Hey!* Calm down!"

I stopped struggling, let out a shaky breath. "Benjy! It's okay, let me go. I thought you were—"

"What's happening? What're you doing?" It was Leanne from the bedroom. Her voice was urgent, a little scared at seeing us like this in her doorway.

"I'm gonna let go now. . ." Benjy said, looking at me as if I was a maniac.

I grinned, both at my own stupidity and at the way he was treating me. "I'm not gonna do anything. Get off me, you heifer."

He released me, stood up and offered his hand to help me up. I could feel Leanne watching us from the darkness of the room, and felt a little embarrassed that she'd witnessed me being outmatched by her

29

boyfriend. Benjy used to be a brown belt at judo when he was younger, and he hadn't forgotten much.

"I thought you were one of the Abbey Cross guys," Benjy said angrily. "You idiot. I heard you pounding up the corridor and about dumped my load."

"You were in the bathroom? Urgh, you weren't. . ." I began, envisioning him using a toilet with no water in.

"No. I was trying to find a cloth to wipe off my shoes." He indicated his shoes, slimed with something black and wet in the darkness. "What were you doing down here?"

"I thought you were –" I said, hesitated for a moment, then finished, "one of the Abbey Cross guys as well." I felt a bit of a mook now, with all my dumb fears about the Catchman put to rest. "I heard you sneaking around down here."

"Hey, you guys, is everything okay?" Leanne piped up from the bed.

"Yeah, it's alright, go back to sleep," Benjy told her dismissively, in a tone that made my blood boil.

She muttered something nasty and lay back on her pillow, staring at the ceiling.

I flicked my butterfly knife closed and latched it, before returning it to my pocket. "Sorry about that," I said.

"You could have had my throat out," he replied, not pleasantly.

"At least you know you've got good sentries in this place," I joked weakly.

"Yeah, lot of good it does me if I get stabbed every time I go out for a leak, know what I mean?"

"That where you were?"'

"Yeah, that's where I was," he mimicked, exasperated.

"Okay. Sorry." ·

"Go back to bed," he snorted.

"Yeah. See ya."'

Benjy didn't bother replying. He stalked into his room and slammed the door, shutting him in there with Leanne.

I was so angry with myself, I couldn't sleep at all for the rest of the night.

4

Another excuse for a dawn dragged its weary way across the city. I woke and munched on one of our supply of Nutri-Grain breakfast bars while Skeet roused himself. We had crates of the things. Dino's mate owned a wholesalers, and between him and Fiver's money, we often found ourselves ending up with slightly out-of-date produce in alarmingly large quantities. Nutri-Grain was the latest thing that Dino had managed to lay his hands on. I was pretty sick of the taste, I'll tell you that.

Our gang was a strange little clump of people, I thought to myself as I ate. More like a commune than a gang, really. Some of us were here because we'd run away from home; some of us lived nearby, but chose to stay at Mos Eisley because of the freedom it offered, and were willing to endure the discomfort of living without luxuries like heating and water. Of course, if we all pulled our weight, we could probably get the electricity and water back on line, but we were too disorganized for that. Besides, we were happy the way it was.

Basically, the linchpin of Mos Eisley was Fiver, and not Benjy, as he would have liked to think. Without Fiver, we'd have had to go out and get jobs, a culture shock which would have caused widespread fatalities amongst our bunch of slackers.

Fiver, like I told you before, was something of an urban terrorist. He knew where to hold a magnet on the side of fruit machines so they always hit jackpot; he knew how to phreak free phone calls, and how to mix thermite from easily obtainable chemicals that could burn through the locks on payphone cashboxes in seconds. He could sucker the guys at the Post Office with a fake address and an old bank book with a slightly altered date. And that was only the tip of the iceberg.

He knew a hundred ways of getting cash, but he insisted on staying strictly small in the amounts he took. The police didn't care about small-time theft, he said, especially the victimless crimes that he perpetrated. He said it was his way of getting what he deserved from the system. I wasn't going to wax moralistic with him, even if I cared enough to bother. He always put nearly all of what he got in the "pool", and that was for everyone.

See, that's what I mean: Fiver took all the risks, but he was prepared to surrender the profits for the common good of our little gang. Everybody was like that. We all had our parts to play.

With Dino, he was the guy with the contacts. He could get the stuff we needed. Win had the car, and parents who were willing to pay her petrol and insurance. Benjy owned the house. I was the guy who basically did everything that needed doing when nobody else wanted to do it, as well as being the unofficial watchdog, as last night had proved. Leanne – well, she was there 'cause she was nice to look at, I guess. A professional girlfriend. And I can't even think of an excuse for Skeet; he was just a blob of carbon and protein that used up our air.

"Are we goin' into town or what?" he said, appearing at my shoulder.

"I've been waiting for *you*," I replied. "It was your dumb idea in the first place; least you could do is bother to get up for it."

"No, the *least* I could do is sit here and do nothing all day," Skeet replied. "Which is what we do every day, and it's gettin' kinda boring. 'Sides, I thought you'd welcome the chance."

'The chance for what? To get my head stoved in by the Abbey Cross lot?"

"You know, with Leanne. . ." he said, letting the sentence hang. I didn't bother to argue it any more. Skeet knew all about my feelings on the subject of that particular girl; this was just his clumsy way of trying to make me look daring and adventurous in front of her. I appreciated the sentiment, anyway.

"Besides, I nicked some shrapnel from the pool," he said, with a grin. "We can drop in the arcades."

"Skeet, my boy, I like your style," I replied, much happier about the whole thing now. I would have felt guilty about stealing cash from the pool for wasting on arcade machines, but since Skeet had done it, I figured it was okay.

34

We wandered into the city centre, making our leisurely way through the old, narrow roads that surrounded Mos Eisley. It was a grey, overcast day, and a chilly wind made it seem a lot colder than it actually was. A standard British winter day, by my reckoning; the clouds overhead looked too depressed to even bother snowing, and they just loafed around idly, making everything look miserable.

"You can't wait for ever, y'know," Skeet said, out of the blue, as we were sloping along the pavement.

"*Duh!* I'm not *going* to wait for ever," I said, instantly cottoning on to what he was talking about. Leanne, of course.

"What I mean is, like, maybe we could be lookin' around for somethin' else," Skeet said, looking a little abashed at making the suggestion. "If it weren't for Leanne, I mean."

I stopped. He walked on a couple of steps before noticing.

"Hang on. What're you saying?"

He shrugged. "Just, it's like, we came to the city, and we fell in with Benjy and that lot, and we just – well, settled. We haven't even looked around for anythin' else."

"You're getting sick of Mos Eisley?" I asked. This was shocking news to my ears. I hadn't imagined that Skeet would ever have the motivation to do *anything*, much less suggest something like – what *was* he suggesting, anyway? I asked him.

"I dunno. There could be more than this, is all. I dunno what. But I reckon we should have a look. I mean, it's not as if Mos Eisley is perfect, is it?"

"What's wrong with it?"

"Not the house. The house is fine. I'm bored of the people, is all. Win and Dino. Fiver's okay, I suppose. But I can't take Benjy much longer, and he kinda comes with the house, don't he?"

I noticed he'd tactfully avoided mentioning Leanne, so I decided to do it myself. After all, that was what was really eating him. "And what, you think it's 'cause of Leanne that we haven't left by now?"

He shrugged. "Well, you are kinda hung up on her. And come on, you gotta be honest with yourself, she ain't gonna break up with Benjy. Not anytime soon, anyway."

I resumed walking, and he fell into step with me. "I wish you'd told me before. That you wanted to leave," I said, sullenly.

"I'm tellin' you now," he replied.

"And this is for definite?"

Skeet shrugged. "Nothin's for definite. All I want to do is check out the options, is all. If I'd known you were gonna take it so hard, I wouldn't have bothered tellin' you."

He was right. I was taking it hard. And he was also right about Leanne. The other guys I could take or leave, but I didn't want to leave her. It'd be like admitting defeat or something. And I was still hanging on to the dumb possibility that she'd give Benjy the flick and suddenly become available.

We walked a little further in silence.

"Hey, you all right?" he said suddenly.

"Course I'm all right," I said. "I just wish you'd told me before, is all."

Skeet frowned. "What're you talkin' about?"

"I wish you'd *told* me that you wanted to go."

"I ain't talkin' about *that*," he said. "You glazed out back there. Didn't you notice?"

"What?" I asked, getting a touch irritated.

"I was *talkin'* to you for about thirty seconds," Skeet went on. "You were in another world. Don't you remember?"

"Remember what? I've been listening to everything you said," I replied. "Not that any of it's worth listening to," I added afterward, making the weak joke more because I felt I should than because I wanted to.

Skeet rubbed his hand over his skinhead, his slack face becoming concerned. "Look, Davey, this ain't the first time. I get worried about you. Ever since you went home last. . ." He stopped, letting it hang. We both knew what he was talking about. I closed my eyes and shut out the memories. "Well, ever since then, you've been doin' this. Fadin' out on me. I jus' think – maybe it hit you a little harder than you let yourself admit."

"I'm fine," I said, unable to understand his problem. "I was listening to every word you said."

"Whatever," Skeet said, shrugging. And we let it drop as we came up to the city centre.

I went to buy a can from a news vendor while Skeet nicked one of the papers from the stand. I tried to persuade him to spend our money on going to the cinema. The Odeon was doing a re-screening of a triple bill of Drew Barrymore movies. Unfortunately, he didn't share my enthusiasm, and no amount of pleading on my part could make him shell out the money.

Instead, we stopped in at the arcades, played some light-gun games. Skeet had run out of credits way before I had, so I was still blasting body parts off zombies when he said: "Check this out. Another one."

"Another what?" I said, nailing a chainsaw-wielding corpse with a single headshot.

He was reading the paper he had lifted from the news vendor. "That's a tragedy," he muttered to himself.

"What?" I asked irritably.

"Look, they've chucked this Catchman story on page four," he said, slapping the page with the back of his hand. "The front page is how some stupid conference went. PM meeting the Saudis, or somethin'. Where's the human interest? Breaks my heart."

He was being flippant, but something in what he said made me frown, and some kind of decayed bat thing got a lucky munch on me while I was distracted.

Cursing to myself, I blew the manky flying rat back to its eternal rest before asking: "What *about* the Catchman?"

"Hang on, I'm reading. Some kid died last night, like the rest of them. It doesn't say who . . . oh yeah, it does. . ." He stopped.

"*What?*" I said through gritted teeth. The suspense was beginning to grate on my nerves a bit.

"Hey, come on," he urged, grabbing my arm and dragging me away from the game. His eyes were suddenly alight with excitement. "Come on!"

"I got two credits left!" I protested. "Ah, you made me miss!"

"In ten minutes, I guarantee you ain't gonna care. Now come *on!*"

He hurried across town, and I followed behind him, bugging him with questions. Of course, just to be annoying, he wasn't answering. I tried to grab the paper, but he snatched it close to him. I was even gonna buy a paper of my own, I was getting so desperate; but he had all the money, and I didn't have a penny on me.

"Look, just *tell* me, all right?" I bleated at him, but he said for the ninetieth time that patience was a virtue and smiled that smug, gormless smile. Forget the Catchman; *I* could have strangled him then and there.

It wasn't long before I worked out where we were heading. I know I shouldn't have been surprised, but it was like, it all suddenly hit me at once, and the realization made me go cold right down to the bone.

He was taking me to Abbey Cross. That, and what I'd seen last night in the graveyard – that was too much of a coincidence. Way too much.

We started seeing the police cars before long. They were everywhere. Not a few gawkers had come along as well, just like us, their curiosity sparked by the story in the paper. A murder, right on their doorstep. They must be loving it, I thought.

Had I really *seen* the killer? Had I really? And had the killer seen me? Leanne's words from last night drifted back to me: *And if it was the Catchman, then Davey's the only one in the city who knows what he looks like.*

"Okay, I get the idea now," I said, as we walked along the Abbey Cross main street. "Just tell me who it was."

He might have been about to. I guess I'll never know, because right at that moment I was shoved from behind and pitched forward on to the pavement. I scraped my palms breaking my fall, and they burned; but I scrambled back on to my feet angrily, and faced my attacker.

It was Jamie Archer and several of the Abbey Cross boys. Me and Skeet were hopelessly outnumbered. I glanced around. There was a police car parked across the road, but nobody in it. What had Skeet been saying, about the main roads being safe? Apparently these guys didn't care.

40

"You've got a nerve," Jamie said, almost trembling with anger.

"Several of 'em, actually," I said, and was rewarded by being cracked around the face with a punch that sent me reeling. Skeet reached out to steady me, but I shook him off.

"S'alright," I said, loud enough for them all to hear. "Jamie here knows that the next time he tries that, he's gonna be picking a blade out of his gut, don'tcha Jamie?"

I was all mouth; I wouldn't really have knifed him. But he didn't know that. Still, they crowded forward at the insult, about ready to lay into me.

"Five of you and two of us. I can only get one of you," I said hurriedly, my hand stealing into my pocket. "Which one wants it?"

They stopped. I don't know how it would have gone then, but I was saved by the return of the cop from the house where he'd been questioning potential witnesses.

"Everything alright, lads?" he called over to us, and the tone of his voice suggested that he knew it wasn't, and he was warning us not to start anything.

Nobody answered him, but I relaxed a little bit and so did they. The cop got back in his car and sat there, watching us.

Jamie Archer glared at me, his square-jawed face set in an expression of naked hate. "We know it was you lot," he said.

Skeet, as usual in a pressure situation, was paralysed and no help at all. I was on my own.

"None of us did anything," I replied quietly.

"You left your tag right in the middle of the cemetery!" Jamie spat.

"Yeah, but we didn't kill anyone," I said, totally serious. "I swear to you, we didn't kill anyone."

Jamie just stared at me.

"Who do you think we are?" I cried, getting bolder because I knew they'd never attack me with the cop nearby. "You seriously think any of us are gonna *strangle* someone? I don't even know who it is you're talking about!"

"Oh, so you just happened to be passing by?" Jamie sneered.

"I knew someone had been killed. I didn't know who," I said, casting a stinging look at Skeet, who looked pitifully back at me, like he was a baby seal about to be clubbed.

"Rob Alder," came the reply from one of the other guys. "You tell Benjy that. As if he didn't know."

I understood now. As if it wasn't bad enough that me and Benjy had been seen in Abbey Cross that night, as if it wasn't *worse* that we tagged the place to prove it ... now the kid who had been killed was Leanne's ex-boyfriend. We had witnesses and we had motive.

But only I had *seen* the killer. I wasn't inclined to try and explain that to them, though. Jamie had just nailed me in the face for starters, and they'd never believe me anyway.

"Listen, Jamie. I'm sorry about Rob. All I can say is I swear we had nothing to do with it. We were here last night, we tagged the cross, but we had nothing to do with this. I know you probably don't believe me, but that's where it is. Come on, Skeet."

With that, we walked past them and away, and they couldn't stop us. I could feel their eyes on my back as I went. I had only gone a few paces when something occurred to me, a final fact I needed to know. Even though I knew I shouldn't, I stopped anyway and turned back to Jamie.

"Where was he killed?" I asked.

Jamie stared at me hard. "Cemetery," he said after a moment.

"That's what I thought," I muttered quietly, turning away. My suspicions had been confirmed. I'd seen the killer, and the killer had seen me. It was the Catchman.

5

Leanne took it pretty hard. There was me, and her, and Benjy, all sitting in their bedroom at Mos Eisley on the double-bed mattress. Skeet had chickened it and protested that he had to go out somewhere. So I was left to break the news. I wanted to tell Leanne in private, but Benjy insisted on being there. Presumably he thought I was gonna try and put a move on her or something; maybe he was a bit suss after catching me outside their bedroom last night.

"Did you see him?" she said, on the brink of tears, her lower jaw trembling. "Did you actually see his body?"

"It was all over the papers, Leanne," I said sympathetically. "And one of Jamie's gang told me himself. It's not a joke or a mistake. It really happened."

I expected Leanne to go hysterical, but she held herself in control. Tears spilled silently down her cheek, or dripped off her cute blunted nose, but she didn't make a noise.

"This is bad, know what I mean?" Benjy said, shifting his weight to get comfortable. "We'd better call Bannon and get him to come over."

"Why?" I asked, puzzled. Bannon was the last member of our gang, a sort of fairweather member who used Mos Eisley as a home whenever he felt like it. He was as thick as a bank vault, but he was also the hardest kid I'd ever known. A proper nutter. Very good in a scrap.

Benjy looked at me. "*Duh!*" he said, using my word, which made me sort of angry. "What d'you think the Abbey Cross guys are gonna do now? They think we've done it, remember? They're gonna be down on us like a swarm. We need everybody we can get."

I couldn't believe my ears. "Hey, can't this wait? At least a little while? Her friend's just died." I motioned at Leanne, who was still weeping silently.

"He wasn't her friend, he was just an ex," Benjy said. "Don't know why she's so bothered about it."

I was about to reply, but stopped myself. I took a deep, steadying breath, and then turned to Leanne instead. "You alright?" I said.

"Course she's alright," Benjy said.

"I was asking *her*," I said, and this time I didn't disguise the anger in my voice.

"I'm okay," Leanne sniffled. I wanted to hug her, not just for purely selfish reasons but also because I felt she needed it. But with Benjy in the room, I just couldn't.

There was silence for a few seconds, during which Benjy watched Leanne, looking faintly disgusted.

"Can't you *stop* that?" he said suddenly. "It's not as if you've seen the guy in the last two years. I dunno why you even care. Get over it, or something."

45

That was it. The words had barely registered in my head before a red haze welled up behind my eyes. I grabbed Benjy by his leather jacket and pulled him to his feet, shoving him away from me. He was too surprised to try any of that judo stuff; but his face crumpled in rage.

"Get out of here," I said to him, the words coming out ironclad. I was making a terrific effort not to say something I'd really regret later. "You're *not* helping."

"Come on!" Benjy growled. "Shove me again. Come on!"

"Can't you be just a *little* bit sensitive?"

"Whaddyou care?" he challenged.

"What does it matter?" I returned.

He laughed suddenly, short and cruel and humourless. "I know what this is about. You think you're gonna get in with *her* like this?"

"Is that what you're thinking about?" I cried. "Okay, let me say it slowly and see if it gets through your stupid skull. Her – friend – has – just – *died*. Amongst human beings that usually calls for a little compassion, get it?"

"You're getting *way* too big for yourself," he replied, threatening. "You need taking down a peg or two, know what I mean?"

"Yeah, well, when I do, it's not gonna be by you."

"Shut *up*!" Leanne screamed at us. "Shut up, *both* of you! Just get outta here!"

Benjy glared at us both venomously, then turned

46

and stalked away. I didn't go. Instead, I closed the door behind him and sat down on the bed next to Leanne. I put my arm around her shoulders. She stiffened at my touch; and then she buried her head in my chest and wrapped her arms around me, and really began to cry.

We stayed like that for a while. Once, the door opened and Fiver popped his head in, but I put my finger to my lips and nodded at Leanne, and he retreated hastily. Eventually, she'd either cried as much as she was going to, or just got bored of it because it wasn't doing any good. Maybe she felt that she should say something to me; after all, I'd been holding her for a good ten minutes. Whatever the reason, she wiped her face on the sleeve of her leather jacket and, still leaning her cheek against my chest, finally spoke.

"I can't believe he did that. I can't believe it. I hate him."

"No, you don't," I said, wishing the opposite was true but not quite believing it.

"I do," she insisted. "Why do I do it? I don't get it. Why do I stay with him?"

"If *you* don't know, I sure don't," I replied.

She smiled. I didn't see it, but I could sort of feel it through my top. I mean – look, I can't explain how I knew, I just *did*, okay? Live with it.

"He's probably gonna kill you for what you just did," she said quietly.

"He's not as hard as he makes out, I said, unworried.

She muttered something softly into the cotton of my camo-green grandad shirt.

"Huh?" I said.

She shifted her face so she could look up at me. "I said thanks," she repeated.

"S'okay."

"You're always really nice to me," she said.

"I'm playing out of character."

"Yeah, sure," she said, smiling and nudging me with her shoulder. "I don't get you guys. Why are you always trying to look mean?"

"Maybe we *are* mean," I said, smiling back.

"Benjy is," she said, sighing, "but you ain't."

"Great," I said. "Now she calls me a candy-ass."

She chuckled. "I won't tell anyone."

I stroked her hair comfortingly. "You really think Benjy's gonna be mad?" I asked after a few moments, already knowing the answer but saying it anyway.

"Oh, yeah. You know how jealous he gets."

"Well, yeah. But I try and sorta stay out of all that."

"Obviously," she replied. "That's why we're where we are now."

"Like I said, I'm playing out of character."

"Yeah, you did say that," she sighed. "Benjy's just – I mean, that's what it was all about just now. He hated Rob. Really hated him. And he'd never met him, ever."

"It was 'cause he was your ex?"

She nodded. "I mean, you know that's why the

48

whole Abbey Cross vendetta got started in the first place. Over me. And it just grew from there." She paused. "He thinks I still fancy Rob, just 'cause I'm upset that he's. . ."

She didn't finish, but I knew what she was saying.

"He's had a go at me before now over you, as well. He thinks the same thing about you. You gotta be careful, Davey. He can get really mad about it."

Ironic, really, how even a mook like Benjy could be cruelly accurate in his perceptions and never even know it.

"I'll bear it in mind," I said.

"It's just – well, stay out of his way for a while. He's wound up anyway about the police and all that."

"What about the police?" I asked, sudden concern.

"Don't you know?" she said querulously, brushing her hair back from her face. "The police came round while you were out. They were asking questions, where we were last night and stuff, but we didn't know what it was about. Then they told us it was about a murder, and 'cause you guys had tagged the place last night someone must have told them about us. I didn't even think at the time, 'cause they never said who it was who'd been done and none of us thought to ask, but – I didn't know it was *Rob*." She nearly began to cry again.

"So what happened?" I asked, momentarily too worried about her story to comfort her.

"I think they might have tried to get someone for

vandalism if they hadn't been more concerned with the other stuff," she said, blinking back her tears, looking a little hurt that I hadn't given her any sympathy. "But you know what we're like: we ain't gonna say anything to the police. They didn't have nothing. Just that you two happened to be in Abbey Cross that night. They said they'd come back, but I don't reckon they will."

I relaxed, and she settled back into me. It was nice, sitting there with her clinging to me. Better than nice. I know it was selfish to think, but let's face it, I'm basically a selfish person. There's something about the warmth of a girl that's better than anything. And she smelled great, too – a really sweet perfume.

I like to think I wouldn't have tried to take advantage of her vulnerability if Benjy hadn't come back in then, but I'm just kidding myself. Maybe it was fate's way of averting what could have been a major mistake on my part. Or maybe it was just really, really bad luck. Either way, the door opened then, and there was Benjy.

He didn't show any reaction when he saw us with our arms around each other. I was plainly comforting her and not doing anything else, but I still fully expected him to lose it. He didn't, though. He just sorta stood there, like he was waiting for me to go so he could talk privately with Leanne.

What could I do? Gently, I eased her off me. She looked resentfully at Benjy, her deep brown eyes bitter. I got up, and walked silently past him. He held my gaze, and I held his, and neither of us were gonna break it off. Eventually, it had to end, because we were both in danger of twisting our heads off as I walked through the doorway; but nobody gave an inch, and we both thought what the other was thinking. I was walking on eggshells with him, and I knew it.

The door closed behind me. It wasn't slammed, but there was something cruelly final in the sound of the wood hitting the jamb, and the spring latch hammering home.

6

My first thought on waking was: *Can't I just get* one *night of uninterrupted steep?*

The second was that there was someone in the room with me. Someone other than Skeet.

I'd come awake without opening my eyes. I don't know how I knew, maybe it was some kind of sixth sense or something, but I was as certain as I've ever been about anything in my life. It was like waking into a nightmare. Because whatever it was that was telling me that there was somebody in my room, it was also telling me – *screaming* at me – that this person was not here to play a joke on me, not someone who'd come into the wrong bedroom by accident, not Leanne come to slip under my covers. It was someone come to kill me.

My skin prickled with goosebumps. I didn't know how much of it was the cold night air and how much was the raw, utter terror that dived down my throat and lodged in my chest like an iceberg. The mountain of blankets that surrounded me constricted my arms, trapping me.

I didn't dare open my eyes. Even though it was dark, I could almost feel the intruder looking at me; and if they saw the wet glint of my eyeball, they would strike. But I couldn't bear it, I *couldn't*.

I heard a soft shuffle near the doorway.

I eased my eyelids open, the narrowest of slits, looking through a fringe of lashes.

It was dark, of course. But the moon was out, free of the clouds that had masked it yesterday, and it shone faintly through the window of the bedroom. Carefully, trying to keep my breathing deep and even though I was practically on the verge of screaming, I tracked my eyes around the room.

There. Standing in the open doorway, framed in the lighter blackness of the landing beyond.

The Catchman.

The realization crashed through me, making me want to run, to cry for help, *anything*. But I knew that one movement would bring him down on me. I knew, under the impenetrable shadows of that heavy cowl, his eyes were trained on my bed.

I tried to focus, tried to bring some definition out of the chaos of fear that was thrashing around inside me. What could I do? What could I *do*?

The hunched form slipped inside, his black habit whispering across the floorboards. I could barely see him, but somehow I had an impression of long fingers snaking from beneath the hem of the loose, hanging sleeves. He came on a few metres, and then stopped, crouching like a mantis, his head held to one side as he watched me. Almost as if he knew I could see him.

He must have known I was awake; I was hardly able to keep my breathing under control any more.

And then I remembered: my clothes were piled next to my bed, where I always threw them. My butterfly knife was in my pocket.

Slowly, I inched my fingers from where they rested against my hip, worming them under the edge of the blankets, feeling for my trousers.

The Catchman seemed to rise and straighten, a reaction to the movement. I froze. He knew! He knew!

And then an idea struck me, desperate and urgent. Mumbling something incoherent, I rolled over in my bed, first to one side, and then to the other, where my clothes were. Dreaming. Or at least I hoped that was how it would appear.

I couldn't see him now; I'd rolled on to my side, and my back was to the intruder. I had to just hope my move had worked. Chill sweat dripped from beneath the matted wads of my hair. I reached out a little further with my fingers, finding the coarse material of my combat slacks, my thumb touching a belt-loop. The pocket was close by. If I could just. . .

I never finished the thought. There was a sudden rustle of movement, and that sixth sense told me to scramble aside a moment before the Catchman fell on me. Somehow, my hand slipped into the pocket. . .

Please let it be the right one, please let it be. . .

It was. The blade blurring, I spun my knife open and stabbed, but there was nothing there but air. He was on top of me, impossibly fast, his fingers clamping on my windpipe. He squeezed hard, strong hands

54

crushing my throat, but I scrambled loose, flailing frantically.

I couldn't seem to hit him. It was like trying to pin an eel, as if he was as insubstantial as the darkness. And I couldn't *see* him; he was like a clot of shadow, just a swirling black mass that my eyes refused to define. His cold fingers were probing again at my throat, one hand trying to fend off my knife arm.

And then I found my voice, and I yelled for help, trying to rouse Skeet, who I knew would be sleeping on the other side of the room.

"What?' came Skeet's voice from the other side of the room, thrashing awake. "What?"

The Catchman pulled off me, drawing back, his cowl whipping this way and that to see if anyone else had heard me. I scrambled to my feet, wearing only my shorts and T-shirt, my knife held out in front of me.

And then he turned and fled, his habit whirling around him like a cloud of ink, escaping across the landing.

I didn't think about what I was doing after that. It had all happened too fast for me to do anything but react. I suppose I just did what I did, maybe because I was angry, or maybe because I was scared, and I didn't want to give in to that.

Whatever the reason, still dressed in just the shorts and shirt that I slept in, I ran after the fleeing figure.

He flowed across the landing, darting down the

stairs. I could barely see him; he seemed to blend into the darkness, so that I had to squint to make him out. It was as if he was only half there; I couldn't bring my eyes to focus on him properly. Too dark. But I went after him anyway, thundering barefoot across the boards, following him down.

I lost him for a second, but a moment later the slamming of the front door told me where he'd gone. I wrenched it open and ran out on to the pavement. Like I said before, I'm a fast runner, but the shadow I was chasing was much faster.

"Hey!" someone cried from inside the house, as I pelted out. I couldn't tell who it was – Dino, probably.

Stray stones from the pavement began to bite into the soft, bare pads of my feet, but I ignored them. I was too caught up in myself, too obsessed with the idea of exacting payback on the scumbag who'd tried to throttle me. The knife in my hand gleamed in the flat yellow of the streetlights. I was gonna *get* him.

I caught a fleeting impression of movement in an alleyway to my left, and I shifted direction to follow. The cold winter air was beginning to set into me now, blasting me with a constant icy gust as I ran. It hadn't taken long. I could feel my fingers and toes going numb.

The alleyway curved on to the park; it formed a path that ran through a side gate and across the wide, moon-drenched grass.

I had a brief impression of the dark figure ahead

before I reached the gate, grabbed it and pulled it open. At least, that was what I had assumed would happen; instead, I wrenched my elbow and shoulder, discovering that the gate was locked.

No way could he have got over it that quickly. That's impossible.

Had he gone through *it?*

No. Dumb. This thing was about as far from being a ghost as you could get. I'd felt his hands on my neck, and they had been real. My throat was still sore from where he had got a grip on me.

I sprang up the gate, negotiating it as easily as I'd cleared the one in Abbey Cross yesterday. Adrenalin had made me surprisingly supple, even when I'd only just woken up. My bare feet hit the cold, dewy grass, slipping a little, and then I was after him again. Picked out in the moonlight, a faint shadow of movement was creeping towards the edge of a nearby copse of trees, their branches rustling in the wind.

I went for them, going full pelt. The footing was bad; my soles were soon slick with dew, and I began to slip against the grass. A faint voice in my head was telling me to give it up, that I was beginning to freeze, that what I was doing was stupid and dangerous. I wasn't listening.

Then I was inside the copse, heading through the trees, letting them close around me, swallow me. I thought I could see him ahead; my eyes were fixed only on him, afraid that if I looked away I'd never be able to find the swirling blackness of his habit again.

And then suddenly he was gone. I came to a halt. I listened. There was nothing.

And I realized how stupid I'd been.

Cold, half-naked and alone, I'd allowed myself to be lured into the middle of this wide cluster of trees. I couldn't have made it easier for him if I'd strangled *myself*.

I began to shiver. Partly it was the temperature; mostly it was the fear. My eyes darted around, looking for him; but all I could see were the blank trunks of the trees, and the clinging shadows that hung between them. All I could hear was the stir of the branches, dry and sibilant, evergreens that had kept their leaves even in the winter. Everything was still. The thump of my heartbeat suddenly became very loud, pulsing just below my ears, as if someone had turned the volume up.

A rustle to my left. I whirled, my dreads whipping round after me. I caught the briefest flash of movement, half-real and half-imaginary, but when I looked after it, it was gone.

I was too exposed in here. The trees provided an angle of attack from any quarter. He could be sneaking up on me, unnoticed right now. He could be *right behind me*.

I spun again, and caught a blurred image of the hooded form of the Catchman before I was knocked

58

off my feet, sent to the cold, wet ground. Panting, I scrambled up again, my knife ready; but I found only the darkness, and the blank boles of the trees regarding me innocently, as if nothing had happened.

My grip was beginning to weaken on the cold metal handle of my butterfly knife. My knuckles and wrists felt feeble, numb. My ears were just curls of dead flesh on either side of my skull.

It was too cold. *Too* cold. And I was vulnerable, dressed in just shorts and a T-shirt, my naked feet slimed with dew and sodden blades of grass.

A twig cracked behind me.

I turned too slow, and a hand snatched my throat, threw me down to the grass again. I hit my head on the protruding root of a tree. Frantic, I turned myself over, ready to face the attack; but again, I faced emptiness.

He was playing with me.

"Come out!" I shouted. "Stop messing around!"

Silence. Then: "Davey?"

Skeet's voice. Nearby.

"In here!" I yelled. "In the trees!"

I didn't drop my guard for a moment. I just kept circling, my knife held out ready, waiting. My eyes were fixed on the dark chasms between the tree trunks. My hand trembled; my jaw was juddering, making my teeth chatter.

"Where?"

"In here!" I shouted again.

Something moved. I reacted instantly, turning to face it, but it was nothing.

A loud rustling from my right. I knew it was Skeet – the Catchman wouldn't make that kind of noise – but it didn't stop me jumping. He emerged suddenly, wearing a heavy overcoat, and his shoes were unlaced on his sockless feet.

"What?" he said, catching my expression, and seeing the way my blade was held out before me.

"Nothing," I said, the words trembling through my chattering teeth. "Let's get out of here. And keep your eyes open."

"Why?"

"Just do."

We made our way carefully out of the copse; and even when we were clear, even though I was practically dying from the cold, I refused to run to get home. I wasn't gonna let the Catchman have the satisfaction. Because I knew he was somewhere, watching us, and I didn't like it.

7

Skeet brought me back to Mos Eisley. Most people were up now, roused by my shout and the chase around the house. Fiver had just lit the fire in the old hearth, and our little camping-gas stove was next to him, boiling up packet soup. I loved that kid right at that moment. It was probably the most thoughtful thing anyone had ever done for me. Certainly Mum would never have thought of anything like that. And Dad – well, forget it.

Skeet sat me down by the fire and Dino appeared with a blanket, wrapping it around my shoulders. I took off my sodden T-shirt and hunkered close to the meagre warmth of the fledgling fire, chattering my teeth.

"It's not much above zero out there, man," Dino said. "You nuts or what?"

"Let him warm up first," Skeet said. "Daft sod was tryin' to turn himself into a snowman."

"Ugliest snowman *I* ever saw, man," Dino said. I was glad *he* was having a laugh; really, I was just loving it right now.

I hugged the blanket closer to me and willed the soup to heat up. Fiver was watching me with concern in his eyes. I couldn't see Leanne or Benjy anywhere, and Win, I was pretty sure, had stayed at her parents' house tonight.

61

Skeet, aware of my discomfort, blew on the fire, but it wasn't doing much good. "We got any turps?" he said.

"There's some white spirit in the cupboard," said Fiver. "It's left over from when they were stripping the house."

"Go get it," Skeet said. Fiver scuttled off to comply, and returned a moment later with the chemical. Skeet took off the cap and filled it with spirit, then chucked it on the fire.

I yelped as a great belch of flame leaped out of the fireplace and blew itself out in my face. Instinctively throwing myself backwards, I escaped with only singed eyebrows. Skeet swore in alarm, but the fire hadn't caught anything.

"You stupid, *stupid* mook," I said slowly, breaking the paralysed silence of the aftermath.

"Got the fire goin', dinnit?" Skeet said. And he was right; the fire was burning heartily now.

After a while, during which the soup finally heated enough to be served to me by Fiver, Benjy appeared in the doorway, followed closely by Leanne. Dino looked up at her as she entered, a faint, hopeful smile on his face; she glanced at him once and then away, dismissing him. I frowned. That wasn't the first time I'd seen them act oddly with each other recently.

"What happened?" Benjy said, looking faintly irate at being woken up.

"Where were *you*?" I asked over my shoulder, without turning around.

"Whaddya mean, where was I? I was asleep, wasn't I? What's been going on? You lot woke me up with all your talking."

"You didn't have to wake *me* up, though," Leanne mumbled petulantly.

"Shut up," he said, then looked back at me. "What happened?" he repeated.

"The Catchman," I said, realizing how dumb it sounded even before the words had passed my lips.

"Uh?" Fiver said.

"The Catchman. He was in my room."

Benjy smirked. "Yeah. Course he was."

I shrugged underneath my blanket, sipping my soup and gazing into the fire. "I never asked you to believe me. You asked what happened. I've told you. Go back to sleep."

I didn't need to look to see Benjy's face harden behind me. He didn't move.

"Okay, stay, but I can do without your sarcasm for the moment," I said, not turning around.

"You're forgetting whose house this is," he said. "You can—"

"*Look*," I snapped, suddenly standing up and whirling around, my soup forgotten behind me. "I'm freezing cold, I'm wet, I've been woken in the middle of the night and I've had some guy's hands on my throat. I'm not in the mood for any of your *crap*, okay?"

63

Benjy's eyes blazed. The air was charged with tension, as everybody waited to see what would happen, hardly breathing.

"Okay. Tell," he said, and sat down with an expression on his face that told me he wasn't pleased about it. Everybody else sat down on the floor. I told them what had happened, leaving nothing out. I was too shaken up to bother making myself look good; besides, I thought that if I did, Benjy would only pick holes in it and shoot me down in flames later.

When I was finished, Fiver was sitting there wide-eyed, Dino had an expression of admiration and respect on his face, Skeet looked as gormless as ever. Leanne looked fretful, and Benjy looked sceptical. No surprises all round, then. If only *one* of my friends was just a *little* bit unpredictable, I'm sure I'd feel much better about knowing them.

"Can I speak now?" Benjy said sarcastically. Was *he* ever getting on my nerves.

"Yes, Benjy, you can," I replied, with an equal measure of sarcasm and a good dollop of condescension in there, too.

"Did anybody else see him?"

"Who, the Catchman?" Fiver said.

"Of course the *Catchman*," Benjy snapped. Fiver shrank back.

"Skeet was in the room," I pointed out.

"I heard Davey shout," Skeet volunteered weakly. I

64

gave him a look that said: *Is that it*? He looked morose. "It was dark. I just saw you runnin' out."

"I heard him shout as well," Dino added. "And I heard running on the stairs."

"Two sets of footsteps, or just one?" Benjy asked.

"I already told you, he ran *quiet*," I said intercepting Dino's answer.

"Uh-huh," Benjy said, sceptical.

"Don't be so nasty," Leanne said, jumping to my defence. "Why would he go pegging off in the middle of the night in his underwear if something hadn't happened?"

"I'll tell you why in a minute," he said. "First, let, me ask you something." This last sentence was directed at me. "You said he got a good grip on your throat. Hard enough to hurt?"

"Yeah. So?" I said.

"Not hard enough to bruise, though, know what I mean?"

Everyone leaned closer.

"He's right, man," Dino said. "No marks on you. 'Cept that big bump on your head."

"That's where I smacked it on a tree root," I said, challenging Benjy with the evidence, "when he went for me."

"So you fell over. Doesn't mean anything."

"He only grabbed my neck for a second!" I cried. "He didn't get a hard enough grip to bruise!"

Benjy smirked. "You know what I think?"

65

"Tell us, please," I said blandly.

"I think it's all up here," he said, tapping a finger on my forehead. I recoiled from his touch, seething at being treated like a kid. He continued regardless. "I think it's just you. I reckon you woke up from a nightmare, and you *thought* you saw—"

"That is possibly the most lame explanation I've ever heard," I interrupted. "You think I can't tell the difference between a dream and reality? I *saw* him, I *followed* him, I *felt* him. He attacked me. Didn't you hear that part of the story?"

"I heard it," said Benjy. "And if it'd been anyone else, I'd believe 'em. But not you."

"Why not?" asked Dino.

"You dare bring that up," I said to Benjy, "and you are *dead*, hear me?"

Skeet backed away. He knew what was coming.

Benjy ignored my warning. "No, I think that while you're trying to persuade this lot, they should know." He changed his tone of address, to include everyone. "Davey's dad's in an institution down in London. He flipped out a couple of years back. They put him away after a farmer found him catching dogs on his grounds, staking 'em down and skinning 'em. He's a fruitloop." He looked at me. "Guess it runs in the family."

My teeth gritted and I glared at him, the veins in my throat standing out with rage. He knew I was gonna spring for him; he was ready for it. But I

66

couldn't beat him head-to-head; he had enough judo training to give me a threading every time. Choking on my anger, I shucked off my blanket and stormed past him towards the doorway. He didn't even look up at me as I passed.

Sucker. The moment I was behind him, I took a two-step run up and planted my knee in the back of his head. I've never seen anyone collapse like he did, as if he was a puppet and someone had just cut the strings. He pitched forward, boneless, almost falling into the fire. Leanne screamed and everyone else just looked stunned. If you can't fight fair, fight dirty. History is written by the winners.

I swear though, what happened next put me off my stride like nothing else. Benjy, who I'd taken to be pretty much unconscious, got up on his hands and knees, shook his head, and *stood up*. His skull must be made of osmium or something.

He turned around. I don't think I've ever seen anyone so angry in my life. It was like he was so mad he couldn't *breathe*. Right then, I knew that I was gonna get smeared across Mos Eisley, and there was nothing I could do about it short of knifing him. And I wasn't gonna do that. Not unless I was really in trouble, anyway.

But he didn't go for me. He just stood there, trembling with anger, his face so red I thought he was gonna start oozing blood out of his pores. Everybody was watching him, unconsciously moving away as if he was gonna explode. Then he began to walk, very slowly, his hands clenched in fists, towards the door. He passed by close to me; I thought he was gonna try and suckerpunch me like I had him. But no, he just kept right on going.

There was a moment of silence after he left, then Leanne hurried after him. I grabbed her arm.

"Don't," I said. "You know what'll happen."

"Get off me," she cried, and the disgust in her voice at what I'd done made me flinch. I let her go. She stormed out of the room after Benjy.

I sat down again in front of the fire. I could feel everyone looking at me. Then, one by one, they silently drifted away.

I sat there for an hour or more, I don't know. I don't hold with watches; me and time don't get along that well. I'd kind of drifted into a half-dream in the soporific warmth of the fire, when a voice suddenly brought me back.

"Davey? You awake?"

It was Leanne. Awareness faded back in.

"I am now," I said. "What's up?"

She walked across the empty room and sat down on the fireside rug next to me. I turned my head to look at her. The ridge of her cheekbone was swollen and purply-blue.

"I know; you warned me," she said.

I couldn't even bring myself to be angry about it. It

had been so pathetically obvious what was gonna happen, but Leanne had gone to comfort Benjy anyway. And she'd got smacked around for her trouble.

"How is he?" I said.

"I think he's a bit concussed," Leanne said.

I snorted back a chuckle. Leanne giggled in response, then we both fell about laughing. It broke the tension. She never could stay mad at me for long.

"He's really not happy about this," she said, after we had calmed down a bit.

"Reckon not," I said. I looked at my feet. "I think, after this, it's about time me and Skeet were moving on."

"Oh no, don't do that!" Leanne said, laying her hand urgently on my arm. "I'm sure he'll get over it; he's not one to hold a grudge."

Sure he's not, I thought. That's why we've been fighting Abbey Cross all this time.

"I don't want to have to be worrying about when I'm gonna get a knee in *my* head every time I turn my back on him," I said.

"It'll be alright. Don't go. I want you to stay."

That was pretty much it. I'd been on the verge of caving in to Skeet's request to get out of there, and then Leanne pulled that on me. Just the way she said it: *I want you to stay*. She might as well have chained me to a post. I was stuck there.

"I wanted to say sorry, anyway," she said, snuggling closer to me. "For snapping at you."

"Least of my worries," I said.

She sighed. "Did you really see the Catchman?"

"Would I lie to you?"

She looked me over. "I dunno. You *are* a guy. That can only count against you."

"That's your embittered side talking. S'not my fault if you've got a self-destructive taste in boyfriends."

"S'pose not," she said, then smiled. "Still, you *are* a handy target."

"Cow."

"You wouldn't like me if I wasn't."

"Who said I liked you?"

"Nobody. I just know."

I stared into the fire for a bit. So did she, leaning on my shoulder.

"Does it hurt?" I asked after a while.

"Probably looks worse than it is. This is a tickling compared to some of his better days."

"I hate it that you stick with him."

"I can't help it. What else can I do?"

"That's the dumbest reason I've ever heard. Why do you stay with him?"

"You wouldn't get it," she said. That hurt more than anything.

"No, I s'pose I wouldn't," I said, shucking her off me and standing up. "I'm going to bed. See you in the morning."

I left her in front of the fire and walked upstairs. It was getting on for dawn, and the light from outside was beginning to dissolve the pitch darkness in mine and Skeet's bedroom. He was asleep on his mattress.

I heard Leanne's voice again in my head: *And if it was the Catchman, then Davey's the only one in the city who knows what he looks like.*

And doesn't that give him just the *best* reason to come after me?

My throat was still killing me from when the Catchman had grabbed it. I lay down and was almost instantly asleep.

8

I couldn't be doing with Benjy hassling me, so I told everyone that I was gonna go into town and see somebody. Benjy hadn't said a word to me all day, but I could tell he was looking for a chink where he could start hassling me about last night – or about Dad. He knew he'd rattled me, and he was still smarting from the blow I'd dealt him. I decided to get out of there before he had time to formulate another way to antagonize me. Trouble was, when I told everyone I was going, he tried to tell me I couldn't. I sighed and said I'd see him later, then wandered off with the sound of his ranting in my ears. People like him deserve all the frustration they get.

I wasn't really heading anywhere; I just wanted a bit of time on my own. The sun overhead was brittle and painfully bright, and the sky was the kind of clear, frosty blue that makes you wanna stand on mountain peaks, one foot up on a rock, and lean on your knee with a retriever by your side. Course, that was only when I looked up; eye level was crowded with old buildings, peeling paint and walls buried under years of half-ripped posters and flyers.

I let my mind go blank as I wandered through the streets of the city, letting thoughts come and go as they wanted. Predictably, the first thoughts past the post were ones of Leanne. I chased them away. I was bored of running myself into the ground thinking about her. It was all I'd been doing ever since I met her, tormenting myself with the hope that she might one day leave the guy who clearly didn't deserve her. No wonder Skeet was getting frayed with me.

The next most insistent thought was too unpleasant to contemplate. Home. I couldn't stand thinking about that for long; it was too fresh in my memory, only a few weeks old. I buried it quickly, and let my mind go blank again.

I was sorta trolling along, looking at the pavement, lost in myself, when I bumped into someone coming the other way. We both yelped in surprise; neither of us had seen the other. It was a girl of about twenty or so, with short blonde hair.

"Sorry," she said, embarrassed.

"S'alright," I said, my words coming out automatically because my brain was occupied with something else. "My fault."

She smiled nervously and walked on. I stood where I was, waiting for a while to let her get some distance before I turned around and looked at her. Her face was still imprinted on my mind. It was uncanny, I s'pose is the word. She looked. . .

No, you're being dumb, I said to myself. But I couldn't take my eyes off the back of her head.

She looked *exactly* like Drew Barrymore.

Now, that was dumb. I mean, I've seen girls who

look a bit like her, or dress like her or wear their hair like her, or something, but to look *exactly* like her – well, she'd have to *be* her.

But she did! She did!

I turned around and began to walk after her. I didn't really even know what I was doing. I just followed her, keeping at a distance so I wouldn't look like a complete maniac, anxious to catch another glimpse of her face. It couldn't possibly have been her.

She went into a shop, this place called Rumblefish that sold all kinds of shoes. I waited, leaned up against the façade of a closed-down newsagents. Eventually she came out, but she turned away down the street without ever looking my way, and I didn't get to see her properly.

Anxious, I sauntered along behind her through the semi-busy streets. It was getting to me a bit now; I wanted to see her face to be *sure*, but I couldn't let myself get seen, or she'd think I was being a weirdo.

She hadn't bought anything from Rumblefish, but she did stop in at Interflora down the road and got one of those big paper cones of flowers, which I thought was unbearably sweet even though I had no idea who they were for. Boyfriend? Mother? Sick relative? Herself? Whatever.

I didn't catch a glimpse as she came out of Interflora either. By now I was getting unreasonably agit about the whole thing. It was like she was doing it on purpose.

What was worse was that the flower shop seemed to be her last port of call, 'cause it was on the edge of the city centre shops. And now she began walking out into the surrounding estates, where the roads narrowed and greenery became more common. I followed after her, cursing to myself, knowing I'd never be able to sleep tonight if I didn't reassure myself that it hadn't been Drew Barrymore I'd bumped into in the street.

She headed into a fairly plush residential area, one of the few that the inner city area had to offer. There weren't many people on the street here; kids were at school, parents were at work. I wondered vaguely what it was that she did, as she rounded a smooth corner created by a curving sandstone wall that ran along the perimeter of the grounds of an old house.

She must have been out of my sight for only a few seconds, but when I turned the corner, she was gone. I walked on a few steps and stopped, looking up the empty street, a sort of puzzled alarm on my face.

"Alright, what's your problem?" said a voice from behind me, making me jump. I turned round, and there she was, stepping out of a little alcove in the wall that led to a small garden gate. I hadn't seen it, but she'd known it was there, being as she lived here. She was holding a small can of chemical Mace up at me. The flowers were held in her other hand.

I didn't reply for a moment; I was too shocked.

"You've been following me ever since you walked into me," she said. "What're you up to?"

"I..." I began, paused, then finished lamely, "I thought you were someone else."

"Sure you did," she said, unimpressed. "Who?"

"Girl I know," I said. That was partially true, at least. Alright, I didn't *know* Drew, but I'd grown up with her on the silver screen.

The most stupid thing was, now that I saw her properly, she looked *nothing* like Drew Barrymore. Not even vaguely. What had I been thinking? *Duh!*

"You'd better turn around and get out of here," she said.

"Yeah, I think I'd better do that. Sorry."

"Not as sorry as you will be if you ever let me get into Mos Eisley again," she rasped scratchily.

"What?" I replied automatically then, harsher: *"What did you say?"*

"Get *away* from me!" she cried, backing off.

"Was it you? Was it you last night? *Was it?"*

"I dunno what you're talking about! Get away from me! I'll use this!" She held up the can of Mace, point blank.

I was an inch from going for my knife, but at the last moment I pulled myself up short. What was I *doing*? Had she really even said what I thought she had, or had I just misheard her? I was strung out and on edge, but was I really gonna stab her in the street because I *thought* she was...

It didn't matter. She'd seen me go for my knife and her finger pressed down on the stud of the canister. I jerked backwards violently, pulling myself out of the range of the spray, but in the process I tripped over the heel of my other boot and fell backward. The anticipation of the back of my head cracking into the stone wall was, if anything, worse than the moment when it came.

9

Awareness. I blinked. There was none of that gradual focusing that you get in films, when someone gets brained and wakes up in a hospital ward, with blurred faces leaning over them. No, I was just awake, like I'd fallen asleep. Except my neck and the back of my head hurt with an insistency that was eye-watering.

The hospital-ward bit was right, though. As I looked around, I saw green curtains closing me in, shutting me off from the silence all around. I didn't have any idea how I'd got here, but I figured it was better than waking up on the pavement.

Unless, of course, the Drewalike had reported me for assault, and I was here under police guard. The thought added another grim aspect to what was already turning out to be a fairly bad day.

There was only one way to find out. That was to go and have a look.

I tried to get up, expecting my limbs to fail me. They surprised me, and held strong. Standing up gave me a few moments of wooziness, but it passed quickly. Maybe I hadn't hit my head as hard as I thought. A little blearily, my skull and neck aching, I pulled back the green curtain and looked out.

My bed was only one of many that stretched along the ward on either side. Tall windows let in grey light, from which I guessed it was still afternoon. I couldn't have been out for more than an hour. Nearby, a door in a windowed partition led out on to a corridor, which was empty at the moment. Only two other beds appeared to be taken in the ward – between me and the corridor – and both of them were curtained off and silent.

No police, then. Good. But there remained the possibility that they might turn up any minute. Maybe the girl hadn't reported me yet. Maybe she'd spent a bit of time in shock or distress before she got rational and decided to call the police. Or maybe she'd just left me, realizing that she'd been a touch hasty in trying to dissolve my eyes with her little canister.

Hang on, though. Wasn't Mace illegal in this country? I wasn't sure, but I *thought* . . . and it would explain why I didn't have a couple of coppers waiting to greet me with a court summons when I woke up.

Well, it didn't matter now. I'd do my recovering at Mos Eisley, thanks. Time to get out of here.

I was just about to pull the curtains fully aside and step outside. I was just about to, but I didn't – because of who I saw through the partition at that moment, stepping into the corridor slowly, like something out of a nightmare. That faceless black hood, the long, sinewy fingers hanging from the enormous sleeves of his habit.

The Catchman.

I caught my breath, my chest locking tight in terror,

and stumbled back on to my bed. Here? How could he be here? This was a *hospital*! There were people around all the—

My thoughts fell into a jumble as I heard the squeak of the partition door opening. He was coming into the ward.

I went cold. If he caught me in here, now – I mean, I could stand and walk, but that was just about it. I was in no condition to defend myself. And what if they'd searched me and found my knife? My face suffused with horror as I plunged my hand into my pocket – and then relaxed as it met the cold metal there. Silently, I drew it out, unfolding it and holding it out before me.

Footsteps, outside. Echoing on the sterile stone floor.

Frantically, I looked around for a way out, but there was only the green blankness of the curtains, with a gap of a few centimetres at the end where I'd left it open. Irrationally, I wanted to close it, as if that would shut out the thing that was stalking me. Maybe I could get out under the hem of the curtain? I envisaged myself ducking underneath it just at the moment those curtains parted, the Catchman finding the bed empty – but no, it was a stupid idea. It'd never work.

I swallowed bile. I was trapped.

There was the sound of a curtain being drawn back, the metal loops snicking softly along its rail.

Possessed by a terrible fear that he was coming in behind me, I swung my eyes left and right quickly, checking my back. No, my curtain was still. It was one of the others.

The Catchman was working his way along the ward.

My breath had seemed to freeze solid, blocking my throat. Panicky plans and outcomes chased each other around my head. What was happening to the occupant of the other bed? I couldn't hear anything except the thudding of my heart.

Another curtain being pulled aside. I jumped, but it wasn't mine.

But it *would* be mine. Next.

My eyes were fixed on the gap in the curtains, through which I could see out. Footsteps, coming closer. Any second now, the black hood would appear there, the long, long fingers – *strangling* fingers – wrapping around the edge of the curtain to pull it aside, and he would come in.

Closer now. Closer. And. . .

I was quick. My blade flashed – but not into the newcomer. Instead it snickered closed and disappeared into my pocket seconds before the ward nurse pulled aside the curtains of my enclosure.

I think it had been the colour. I had been expecting black, and she was wearing white. If it had been dark blue, I thought with a shudder, I might have knifed her out of reflex, I was so scared.

"You're up. What's the matter?" she asked. She was

a plain-faced, scrawny girl in her mid-twenties with mousy brown hair.

"Nothing," I said, forcing the fear from my face.

"Do you feel alright? You had a nasty knock."

"It hurts a bit," I said. "I'll be okay. Can I go?"

"You can go any time you like. But I'd really like to do some checks first. For concussion, and so on.

"I'm alright," I insisted, sitting down on the bed. Then, as an afterthought, I asked: "How did I get here?"

"Someone phoned an ambulance from a payphone," she said. "Didn't leave a name. Good Samaritan, I suppose. Lucky for you."

"Yeah," I said, relaxing a little. So the Drewalike hadn't called the cops. But that didn't mean she wouldn't, after she'd had time to think about it. And the Catchman was still here, somewhere. I had to get out.

"I'd like to ask you some questions," she repeated, patiently. "Just to check for concussion."

"It's the twentieth of January, the Queen is Elizabeth the Second, and my name is. . ." I paused. "Andrew Barrymore." She looked at me oddly. "Happy?" I said. "I can think straight. Now can I go?"

"If you don't mind staying for just a few minutes, I'd like to bring in a doctor, just to ascertain whether or not you might need an X-ray," she persisted. When she saw me looking sceptical, she said: "It really was a nasty knock."

I decided it would be easier if I just agreed. The moment she was gone, I could get out of here. She nodded and closed the curtains again, once more leaving just a crack.

I watched that narrow sliver of the outside world. At first her thin body and face filled it, then it moved away.

Then a black shadow lunged across it, after her.

I yelled, leaping up from the bed and tearing the curtains aside, trying to warn her about—

She was looking at me oddly, a sort of sympathetic puzzlement on her face. There was no sign of the Catchman. Someone from one of the other beds shouted at me to shut up.

"Please lie down," she said. "It was a *very* nasty knock."

I mumbled something in answer and went back to my bed, confusion on my face. I was *sure* I'd seen something – but there had been nothing there. It was the same thing as with the Drewalike. What was *up* with me?

The sound of the partition door closing was my cue to look outside again. I hesitated for a moment at the curtain, fearing what I might see, and then I pulled it open.

The ward was empty.

I didn't want to stick around a second longer than was necessary, so I quickly crossed to the door and glanced each way up the corridor. I caught a glimpse of the nurse turning down a side-passage; but otherwise there was nobody in sight.

I headed the other way. The soreness in my head and neck was diminishing a little as the muscles loosened up with my movement, but not enough so I didn't wince whenever I turned to look behind me. My footsteps seemed to be the only ones in the building, a hollow echo that disappeared off down the empty corridors.

Nervously, I hurried onward. Doors and corridors passed me on either side, but nothing emerged to break the eerie sense of desertion that seemed to press in on me. Or the sense that there was someone behind me, following, disguising their footsteps by keeping their pace the same as mine.

I passed an elevator, and thought immediately of going down and out of the reception area. But no, I didn't want to be seen. And if there *were* any police on the way, they'd be coming up from that direction. I turned away, looking for an alternative.

The fire stairs.

Motivated by the idea, I hustled down the corridor to the blank white door at the end, pushed the bar down, and went through.

Perfect. A stairwell, one of those zig-zag ones that descends and then folds back on itself until it gets to the bottom. I could see down a few levels through the space in between the stairways, and there was nobody in sight.

Wasting no more time, I headed down. My neck protested as it was jarred by my descent, but right now I was more concerned with getting out of there before the police turned up. Or before—

I swore under my breath, stopping dead and looking upward. Above me, coming from the level I had entered the stairway from, I heard the squeak of the door opening and closing. I squinted. Above me, I caught sight of something black darting across, and then the sound of footsteps. Fast. Coming down.

He's still after me!

Caution thrown to the wind, I flew down the stairs, taking some of them two at a time and jumping down the last few. My head and neck were screaming searing agony at me, but I couldn't help that. Behind me, the footsteps were thudding after me, gaining. I was beginning to feel weak and woozy. Maybe I hadn't been as strong as I thought.

Not here, not now! Hold out! You can't give in!

I thought of the feel of those clammy hands on my neck, those fingers around my throat, and I pushed the pain and weakness to the back of my mind and pelted headlong towards the ground floor. Steps rushed by beneath me, merging into a white blur. Fire escape doors watched me fly past at each flat section. It was a miracle I hadn't tripped yet, but I didn't dare slow down.

What I did dare was to look up as I hit the flat bit of the landing before the next set of stairs. I caught a glimpse of an arm as it held on to a banister, propelling its owner downward; and the arm was robed in black, and the fingers were long and vicious. . .

. . .and he was right behind me.

I put my head down and concentrated on running, but by now I had tuned into the sound of the Catchman's footsteps, and they were getting louder. I had to stand and fight, I had to do *something*, I—

I tripped, my foot missing the last step of a stairway and falling further than I had expected. Unbalanced, I flailed to stop myself crashing to the ground.

I sensed rather than saw the thing behind me as it rounded the corner and tore down the stairs. But I heard his footsteps end abruptly as he lunged at me. That was the last thing I *did* hear, though, because I'd already shifted my momentum to send me barrelling into a fire escape door. I slammed into it, my full weight hitting the release bar and throwing it open before me . . . and I fell through, sprawling on to the smooth, cold floor of a corridor, turning and throwing the door shut behind me.

I had landed at the feet of a pair of nurses, one of whom was attending a patient in a wheelchair. They looked at me in amazement. I didn't care. Scrambling to my feet, I fled towards the elevator. Forget the police; if they caught me instead of that *thing* following me, I'd count myself lucky.

10

The sky began to darken again during the late hours of the afternoon. It kinda makes me ashamed to admit it, but I was beginning to dread the coming of night. There was something that told me this wasn't all over yet.

I'd resolved not to tell anyone about the hospital. Except maybe Skeet. One reason was that I could do without giving Benjy another excuse to lay into me, but also, the whole incident had seemed so strangely dreamlike that I was beginning to doubt my own memory. Had the Catchman really been there? Had he followed me? Or was it all a product of that concussion?

No, the concussion had nothing to do with it. I'd been getting odd flashes of weirdness ever since – well, ever since I went home. I supposed I still hadn't quite got over that. But – I mean, what was I doing? If I was questioning my own state of mind, I was either being seriously stupid or there was something very wrong.

Benjy had us doing patrols that night. We'd never done anything like that before. He set us up at stations around the ground floor of the house, after checking all the windows to make sure nobody could get through that way.

Me, Skeet, Bannon and Fiver were to take the first half of the night; Dino, Win, Benjy and Leanne the second half. Everybody grumbled about it, but Benjy laid down the law: if anyone didn't like it, tough. That also went for anyone who – like Win and Bannon – could still crash at their parents' house. Nobody was leaving tonight. He wanted everyone in one place where he could see them.

So there we were, in the silent, dark house, with only the burning fire for light and a couple of torches that Fiver had nicked. Him and Bannon were doing the outside perimeter, with the torches; me and Skeet had to watch inside. Of course, that meant we just ended up sitting by the fire, drinking Cokes and talking. Nobody took Benjy as seriously as he thought they did. And we certainly didn't live in fear of his orders.

"This is stupid," Skeet said. "This whole thing's goin' sour. Why don't we get out of it, Davey?"

"I *wanna* get out of it," I said. "It's just that – I dunno, it was *me* that nearly got killed last night, remember? Maybe he's after *me*. I mean, it was me who saw him. It's me who he *saw*. He could have followed me back from the graveyard that night. I might have *led* him here. . ." I paused, realizing the implications of what I had just said. "Until we know what's going on, there's strength in numbers."

"That ain't the real reason and you know it."

"Yeah, I know."

Skeet scratched the laces of his shoes, running his finger up and down the intertwined patterns. "I'm not gonna hang around much longer," he said. "I'm not gonna stay just 'cause you've got a dumb crush on this chick."

I was silent.

"I think I know who it is," Skeet said suddenly. I knew immediately what he was talking about.

"You *what*?" I exclaimed. "Who?"

He paused, seeming to think, and then spoke tentatively. "It *could* be Benjy."

"Get outta here!" I said, but I was fascinated. "Why?"

"Don't get me wrong," he said. "I mean, it's jus' an idea. There's no reason it should be someone we know. It's far more likely to be some mook we've never even met."

"Yeah, but – tell me, anyway, Skeet. I wanna know."

He looked at me askance, as if a little thrown by my eagerness.

"*Okay*. That first night you were at Abbey Cross, you lost Benjy, right? Then later on you saw that guy, the Catchman or whatever. And the next thing anybody saw of Benjy was when he got back to Mos Eisley, sayin' he'd been chased off. The same night, Rob Alder gets killed. And Rob Alder was Leanne's ex, wasn't he? And Benjy is, y'know, the jealous type."

"Go on," I said, sensing there was more. I was

captivated in the firelight, the shadows shifting and dancing on my face and playing over my dreads.

"Or maybe he didn't kill Rob then; maybe it was, like, later that night. You told me you caught him coming back in sometime early in the morning."

"Yeah!" I said. "He had something on his shoes; I dunno, it could have been mud, but it might not have been. He said he'd been out to go to the toilet, but. . ."

Skeet stared. I could see the cogs in his head making connections. I went on, feeding his theory.

"Yesterday, me and him had an argument. It boiled down to being about Leanne. He ended up storming off while I stayed with her, but he was mad, right? Really mad. And then, that night, what happens? The Catchman goes for *me*!"

"Yeah, *yeah*," Skeet enthused, getting excited. "And remember, he wasn't around when me and you got back into the house after you chased the Catchman off! Him and Leanne turned up later!"

"I've asked Leanne about that. She says he woke her up after he got dressed. But what if he'd already *been* dressed? I mean, he had a load of time to double back to the house, come in the back way, and get rid of his cloak or hood or whatever."

I thought of the hospital, and decided against mentioning it to Skeet. He'd been worried enough about me 'cause I'd been blanking out recently, like on the way to town. I didn't want to heap further troubles on him.

90

Benjy as the Catchman! I'd been thinking about it in dribs and drabs for a while now, but it was as if Skeet had just dropped a handful of jigsaw pieces on the floor and they'd fallen in perfect arrangement. Of course, I knew the idea was ridiculous. Trying to reconcile the stocky form of Benjy with the tall, lean, cloaked figure was laughable.

But *Leanne* didn't have to know that. Only I had ever seen the Catchman properly. What if I could lead her to believe that *Benjy* was the Catchman? Then she'd have to leave him.

I looked at Skeet closely. Best to keep him out of the picture. What he didn't know, he couldn't give away, and he wasn't the best guy at keeping secrets. The fact that Benjy knew about my dad was testament to that.

Skeet had no idea of the thoughts that flashed across my head in that moment. Instead, he was musing on what I had told him. "But if it is him, if it really is Benjy . . . he's *right here* in this house. With us." He had begun looking over his shoulder at the darkened doorway behind us, rubbing his shaved head anxiously.

"It could just be us being paranoid," I said pretending to try to ease his nerves, knowing that it wouldn't work. "I mean, it's not as if *I* haven't done it before. You know me – seeing patterns where there aren't any, always off on one theory or another."

"No, but this one feels *right*," Skeet said, and I could

91

tell by the worry in his voice that he wasn't gonna be persuaded otherwise. We sat there in silence for a while.

"We gotta go," he said eventually. "Like, we gotta go *now*. This ain't worth it."

"We *can't* go," I hissed.

"Oh, not *again*. Is this because of—"

"Yes, it's because of Leanne, alright? And this is nothing to do with how I feel about her or any of that. It's to do with this: right now, she could be sleeping next to a killer!" I looked at Skeet, my eyes hard. "What am I supposed to do, leave her to be the next one?"

"Yeah, that's *exactly* what you should do!" Skeet returned.

Our eyes met and locked for a moment, then I looked back into the fire, indicating that I was immovable. I could hear Skeet's snort of disgust as he walked away from me.

I sat there for a long while, gazing into the fire, feeling its heat on my face. Eventually, the warmth made me drowsy and that, added to the fact that I'd had next to no sleep last night, made me drift off without even knowing it.

i'm dreaming again but this time i'm not in a metal forest where i might get rust fever but at the bottom of a hill and a long winding path goes up to the house kinda long and winding and it passes through these old crumbling gates and the house is like really huge and distorted and frightening like something out of a horror house movie or psycho or something which makes me smile 'cause it's so cheesy it's funny

so i start walking up this path 'cause i know that's what i'm supposed to do and i'm walking up this hill with all sorts of gravestones on either side of me towards the ramshackle house at the top and i'm wondering how it can possibly stand up 'cause its roof is bigger than the foundations and it's looming forward like it's gonna fall on me

i realize that it's actually been kinda sunny and nice up till now that's the way it is with dreams you don't notice something until you need to and the only reason i notice that it's been sunny is because it's suddenly gone very dark and cold and my jokey mood is gone and now i'm not feeling so good

and i look at the house and i recognize the front door and i know now that it's my house not mos eisley but my parents' house where i grew up and i know that i'm gonna find something really bad inside and i'm terrified but i can't stop myself walking up to the door and i'm suddenly struck by this horrible knowledge that there's someone inside someone who's not my parents and i know who it is i know it's the catchman but i can't stop my hand as it closes on the doorknob and turns it and the door swings open

I only realized I'd been asleep when the scream shattered my dreams and I jerked violently awake. My first thought was that the fire hadn't died much; I

93

couldn't have been asleep for long. A moment later I was on my feet, running to investigate the cry. I was sure it hadn't been Leanne. *Please* don't let it have been her. . .

Not Leanne. Win. It was coming from Win's room. A blubbering wail of grief that sawed through my nerves.

I knew what I would see even before I got there. Win was kneeling next to the bed, screaming at the top of her lungs and rocking back and forth. And then there was Dino, the covers pulled down to his waist, his arms spreadeagled and his eyes open and blank, staring at the ceiling. His tongue was hanging slack out of the side of his mouth. Livid blue bruises formed a collar around the paling skin of his neck.

He was dead.

"Alright, *alright*!" Benjy shouted as he came in behind me. "Shut *up*! What is it?"

Nobody needed to answer him, 'cause his eyes fell on Dino then, and he went white. The others ran in one by one, slowing and stopping as they saw what had happened, until all six of us stood silently around the bed like funeral mourners, watching Win cry uncontrollably over the body of her dead boyfriend.

"Is no one gonna *help* her?" Leanne cried, shoving her way through us. She knelt down next to Win and put an arm around her, muttering platitudes. Win clung to her and wailed, and Leanne glared reproachfully at all of us for being so uncaring.

To be honest, I was still so skittled by the whole thing that I didn't know *how* to react. I think it was pretty much the same for everybody else.

"I w-w-was only g-gone for a *minute*," Win howled.

In the bare room, in the faint light from outside, we all unconsciously hung our heads.

"Now what is *this*?" Benjy snapped. "Tell me what happened! Weren't you lot supposed to be watching out for this?"

We were standing around the fire in the living area. Only Leanne had stayed with Win; the rest of us hadn't been able to get out of there fast enough. My eyes had wandered to the cluster of insulated wires that bristled out from one corner of the wall, hoping one day for an adapter and a home entertainment system to justify their presence. Or even a bit of electricity. But now Benjy had spoken, and my attention was back with him.

"You lot were supposed to be watching inside," he said to me and Skeet. "Didn't you see anything?"

"Would you believe me if I had?" I replied churlishly, digging at him for last night, when he stubbornly refused to accept that the Catchman had been in my room.

"There's someone *dead* in there, Davey. Don't be flip," said a flat voice, and I was shocked to find that it was Skeet's. That put me in my place; it's a rare day indeed when Skeet says something like that to me. He looked sorta wasted, blown away by the whole thing. He'd never seen a dead body before. It was nothing new to me, though. As far as corpses go, Dino's was a PG. You should have seen what Mum looked like after Dad had finished with her.

"We were patrolling all the time," I lied. "Didn't see a thing." I knew Benjy would kick up if I told him we'd been sitting by the fire all night, and I didn't want to give him an excuse.

"Win said she went out to go to the toilet. Did any of you see her?" Benjy demanded after a few moments, ignoring what I'd just said.

"I did," Fiver piped up weakly. He was on the verge of tears. "She was going out round the back of the alley."

"And neither of *you* saw her?" he asked of me and Skeet. "I thought you were supposed to be patrolling?"

"Sorry, Boss," I said sarcastically. "Guess you can dock my wage."

Benjy glared, but he had other things on his mind right now, so he let it pass.

"So in the space of the – what, five minutes that she was gone, someone got in and strangled Dino?"

"Looks that way," said Bannon. "'Less she did it herself."

That brought us all up short. Bannon was never the

epitome of tact at the best of times, but that little nugget surpassed everything.

"Perfect time, innit?" he said. "With all this other stuff goin' on. Was gonna happen sooner or later."

"Why?" someone asked; I think it was me.

"Ev'ryone knows what Dino's bin like with Leanne. Win jus' thought—"

"*What's* he been like with Leanne?" Benjy growled.

Bannon looked dazed for a moment; he always looked like that when he was thinking. "*Ev'ryone* knows," he repeated.

"*I* don't," Benjy replied. I could tell he was getting angry, but he was holding himself in check. The one thing worse than a mad Benjy was a mad Bannon. Getting him riled was not a wise move unless you liked your food through a straw.

"What, not about him cracking on to her an' all?"

Benjy began to redden, his eyes darkening.

Bannon laughed suddenly. "I can't believe you din't know. He was goin' all out for 'er. Win told us. She knew about it. She weren't happy that her boyfriend had eyes for someone else. Don't think Leanne were much pleased, either."

Judging by our faces, it seemed Bannon was the only one who knew what he was talking about. Actually, now I think about it, Fiver did look kinda guilty as well. It did explain the funny looks Leanne and Dino had been exchanging recently; but it was still pretty much a bombshell, and none of us spoke

97

for a moment until Benjy said, "I'm glad he's dead, then. Saves me a job."

And with that he stalked away, leaving us all stunned at his comment.

11

It was gonna be a long night, that much was obvious. And it was far from over yet.

The first problem was what to do with the body. I would have thought it was fairly straightforward, really – call the cops and tell them what happened. None of us wasted much love on the police, but there wasn't really a whole lot of choice. Dino still got on well with his parents; he'd be missed sooner or later if he didn't return.

Bannon advanced the theory that we should leave him somewhere he'd be found, like on the steps of a church or something. I mentioned that the only one of us who could drive was Win, and she'd be less than happy at the idea, even if she was in any state to do it. Bannon pointed out that Benjy could drive too, he just didn't have a car. I said he'd still have to get the keys off Win, and she wouldn't have any of it.

Skeet and Fiver were just sorta blown away by the whole thing; they were numb, not really saying anything. That left me and Bannon, but I could run rings round him. Eventually I volunteered to go to a payphone and call the police.

"You're not going anywhere," Benjy said from the doorway. He had a knife in his hand.

My own blade was out in a flash, an automatic reaction.

"Calm down, Davey," he said. "The knife isn't for you. Protection, know what I mean? But, nobody's going anywhere. We're all staying right inside this house."

"What're you gonna do – leave Dino there to rot?" I cried.

"We talk about it in the morning. The cops already think we had something to do with Rob Alder; if they find Dino here, me and you'll look guilty enough to be sent down. So we wait till morning. Till then, nobody leaves. We stay together. One of us is dead now; there could be another if we all split up."

"So what happens in the morning?" I asked.

"You, and me, and Bannon, Skeet and Fiver," he said indicating each of us in turn with the blade of his knife, "we go to Abbey Cross. And we settle payback."

"You think it was Jamie Archer?" I cried in disbelief.

"Him or one of his gang," Benjy said. It was only then that I noticed he was really, really mad. Normally he goes red and livid, but this time he was kinda quiet and controlled. The result was the same, though; he wanted blood.

I ran my hand distractedly over my dreads. "Uh-huh. You realize, of course, that you've got totally *no* evidence for this."

"Get it together and *think*," he spat. "It's the most obvious revenge attack I've ever heard of. Alder gets

100

killed. Jamie thinks it's us. He tries to get you and fails, so he tries Dino. Evens the score. Make *sense*?"

"Okay, how about this?" I retorted. "Crazed psychopath tries to kill me 'cause I saw him at the scene of Rob Alder's death, fails, then realizes that hey, there's eight kids living on their own in an empty house and wouldn't it be the *easiest* thing to start offing them?"

"Read my lips," Benjy sneered. "There ... is ... no ... Catchman. *Got* it?"

I was about to make a reply, but I checked myself. Instead I said wearily, "You think what you want."

Benjy glared at me. "First thing in the morning," he repeated.

I didn't want to be around him any more. I went to check on Win and Leanne.

"Where you going?" Benjy challenged as I walked out of the living room, putting my knife away, my face falling into shadow as I turned away from the flickering firelight.

"I'm gonna look in on Win," I said, my tone of voice daring him to stop me.

"Be back here in five," he said. "We keep the patrol going till the morning, know what I mean?"

"Whatever," I replied noncommittally.

"I said be back in *five*!" he shouted after me.

I went through the dark hall, and up to the doorway of Win and Dino's room. For a moment outside, I hesitated, listening. Then I went in.

Leanne was in there, Win's head cradled in her lap. Win was asleep, having cried herself into exhaustion. Dino's body was still on the bed, covered up by a blanket. Leanne looked up at me, her expression both sad and grim. Without a word, she slipped out from beneath Win's head and gently lowered it on to a pillow she pulled from the bed. Then she stood up and came over to me. "Come on," she said quietly, and left the room. I followed.

She led me into her room, where we both sat down on the double-bed mattress after shutting the door behind us. It was dark in there, and I could see her only as a bluish tinge as the night-glow struck the curves of her face. The bruise that she'd suffered at Benjy's hands was invisible here.

"I'm scared, Davey," she said. "Really scared."

"I know," I said.

"Aren't you?"

"Course I am," I replied.

"Benjy isn't."

"Yeah, well," I said, then changed the subject. "So what was the story with Dino?" I asked.

Leanne shrugged. "I dunno. He was trying it on with me, I s'pose. He'd get slimy whenever we were alone, but I was having none of it. I don't think he cared much about Win; he didn't really keep it a secret from her. *Ugh.*" She shivered. "I know it's, like, wrong to speak ill of the dead or something, but I really hated him."

102

I shrugged. "He ain't gonna hear now, is he?"

She looked morose. "You don't know that. Don't be a cynic."

There was silence.

"Did Benjy know?" I said.

More silence.

"You reckon it's him, don't you?" she asked softly from the darkness.

"No, I—" I began, but she cut me short with a snap.

"Oh, *Davey*, I thought you knew me better than that. Don't lie. I know you think it's him. S'written all over you."

I hesitated before answering. It wouldn't hurt my cause to play along with her mistake. After all, it was deception intended for a good end. She'd be better off with me than him and we both knew it; she just needed a helping hand.

"Alright, so I think it's him," I said. "I don't *know* it, I just think it. I mean, first Rob, then me, and now Dino. All guys that Benjy had reasons to be jealous of." I paused then, for reasons of conscience, added: "Course, it could easily be coincidence."

"I've been thinking about it myself," she said. "I think it's him, too."

"Then let me get you *outta* here," I replied instantly. "Me, you and Skeet. It's not safe."

I could hear her sigh, see the blue outline of her head dip in resignation. "It ain't something I can do," she said.

"Why *not*?"

"I daren't," she said. "I daren't leave him. He'd find me."

I knew that wasn't much of a reason; she was just coddling my feelings, trying to keep me on the hook. She stayed with him 'cause she couldn't help herself. I didn't even reckon she truly believed it was him that was doing the killings. I was about to argue, but she spoke again almost instantly, changing the subject with indecent haste.

"Everyone's messed up about this," she said. "About Dino. Except you."

I shrugged, but she couldn't see it in the dark. "It isn't just me. Bannon doesn't care a toss, I don't think. And Benjy's hardly in tears about it."

"Bannon's too stupid to care and Benjy's – well. . ." She left it hanging. "So what about you?"

"I've seen worse. The first one is always the bad one, people reckon."

"You've seen worse? When?"

Once more a silence, broken only by the sounds of our breathing in the blackness.

"Okay, here's the story. You know my dad was institutionalized a time ago?"

"Yeah, I remember Benjy said, just before you lamped him with your knee," Leanne said disapprovingly.

"Deserved it," I replied. "Skeet let it slip a long while ago, when he and Benjy got on better. But there was stuff I didn't tell anyone. Only Skeet knows about it, really. See, I left home about, what, a year ago or more. Never really told you why, did I? It was 'cause my dad was coming home. They were closing the institution he was in. Cutbacks and stuff. Anyway, I knew how he could get, and I didn't wanna stick around. So I left."

"Didn't your mum want you to stay?"

"She didn't care either way. I never really had any love for her. I dunno what I did; maybe it was something when I was young. But she never bothered about me for as long as I could remember. And even when Dad was nuts, he was still the only one she cared about."

I could feel Leanne looking at me sympathetically.

"A coupla weeks ago," I began, "I decided I was gonna go back and look in on Mum, see how she was."

"Yeah, I remember," she said. "You disappeared for a day, and when you got back you were awful quiet for about a week. Had me worried."

"Sure it did," I said, with a half-smile. She was gonna protest, but I kept on going. "Anyway, so I got the bus back home for the day. I got back to the house, and nobody was answering; but we always kept a spare key under the plant pot in the garden. I walked right in there and found my mum and dad in the kitchen. He'd stabbed her with a bread knife and then cut his wrists open."

I couldn't begin to describe the scene to her; I

didn't have the words. But I can remember the smell, stronger than anything. Sickly sweet, choking waves of scent that clawed down your throat and nose and never really came out again. And I can remember the blood, dark and arterial, more of it than you could possibly imagine would fit in two human bodies.

I heard her draw in a short gasp in the darkness as I finished my story.

"I know it doesn't happen with everyone," I said "But some people they shouldn't ever let out. They should never have let *him* out, and they *knew* that. But they just couldn't afford to keep him. Priorities, huh?"

"That's awful," she said. I reckon it was the only thing she could think to say.

"Happens," I replied, then I sorta laughed. "He used to hallucinate all the time, before we put him in the institution. He'd think bats were attacking him from the ceiling in his bedroom. We'd find him running around, trying to swat 'em away. He'd actually throw himself to the ground, thinking he'd been knocked down by a giant one, and he'd swear he'd been bitten, even when there were never any marks on him. You couldn't persuade him different. He thought they were really there, and he really thought he felt it when they knocked him around. Pretty severe stuff, all in his head."

I heard a rustle of clothing in the darkness, and then her arms wrapped round me and she was hugging me.

At the same moment, the door to the room opened

and Benjy was standing there. We were caught in the faint light that spilled in from the corridor through the back door window. All I could see of Benjy's face was the glitter of his eyes.

"Seems this is happening more and more," he said, as Leanne slid guiltily away from me. "I said five minutes, Davey. Get out here."

Benjy had us all on patrol again, two inside and two outside while the girls and him slept. This time, he insisted that neither person of each pair should leave the sight of the other. Naturally, I ignored his orders. I don't go well with orders, and I'll only obey someone I respect. I didn't have any respect for Benjy; in fact, it was fast turning to loathing. But he was the default leader of the group because he owned Mos Eisley, and getting myself ejected from the gang was hardly gonna improve my chances of getting Leanne.

The air of paranoia inside was getting too stifling, though. I couldn't take it. There was this gloomy fog of persecution hanging over the inside of the house. First me and then Dino; we knew that someone was out to get us. And Skeet and Leanne weren't the only ones who had theorized that it might be Benjy; I had a feeling Fiver had come up with a similar theory, by the way he looked at our glorious leader whenever he came into the room. It really didn't take much effort on my part to make Benjy look like the Catchman; he was doing it all himself.

So I went out to think myself in circles, just like everybody else was (except Bannon, for whom circles or even basic geometry was an alien concept). There weren't gonna be answers, at least not yet. But I did feel sorta guilty, because at least half of me thought it was my fault, that I'd led the *real* Catchman here from the graveyard – and like I said to Benjy, weren't we just like fish in a barrel, a bunch of teenagers all alone in this big, empty house in the middle of no-one-cares?

So anyway, I decided to get outta there for a bit. I told Skeet I was gonna dart and asked him to cover for me.

"Natch," he replied, drearily unenthusiastic. He was still sore that I wouldn't leave this place without Leanne. I left him to get on with being tired and miserable and wandered out the back door, avoiding Fiver and Bannon on patrol with ease. Nobody cared enough to bother adhering very rigidly to Benjy's orders, especially as he had volunteered himself to be the one to get some sleep, 'cause it was his house.

Outside, the temperature was much the same as it had been last night, except this time, I was wrapped up warm against it. It had a sort of crisp, brittle edge, just on the verge of frosting. My breath steamed the air as I stepped out the back door.

Behind Mos Eisley, a little cobbled alley ran along, leading on to other back doors and garages, a narrow channel between the clotted houses. Stairways led up

108

to first-floor apartments. Clouds lumbered by overhead, dark and invisible in the night.

A cat, a stout white tom, was watching me from the low wall of a neighbour's property. I walked over and sat down on the little step below him, that led along a short concrete path through our neighbour's back yard. The cat dropped silently down and began gently butting my legs with its head; I stroked it absently, tickling under its flea collar.

It was better outside. More peaceful. This whole Catchman business had got us all so on edge that we were about ready to fall apart, and our gang had never been as tight and organized as Jamie Archer's anyway.

I found myself thinking about us, the gang. What was really tearing us apart? Was it the murders? Well, that was the most obvious answer, but I didn't think it was the right one. It was the myth: the urban myth of the Catchman. Because if what was stalking us was just a man – well, that was something that could be overcome. A single man could be beaten.

But he had become something more in all our minds – in the minds of the whole city. Something huge, something *unstoppable*. And it was that fear, that uncertainty that disarmed us, made us weak, even though we all knew it was stupid – he was *just* a man. But I don't think any of us, no matter how hard we tried, could really say we were *certain* of that.

This city bred its own kind of paranoia. The

Catchman was as much a part of the city as the city was of *him*. And now he was picking us off, one by one.

I looked at the cat. "I'll bet *you* know what's going on."

The cat narrowed its eyes smugly at me.

"Thought so," I said.

A moment later I heard a noise, and I saw something move out of the corner of my eye. I reacted instantly, scrambling behind the low wall of the neighbour's yard and pressing my back against it, my knees drawn up to my chest. The cat disappeared like a genie.

It was probably only my reactions that saved me from being seen. The noise had been innocuous enough; it could have been one of a million possibilities. But I knew what had made that noise by the sudden wave of dread that swamped me.

Sitting motionless behind the wall, I peered out until I could see right down that alley – and I saw the Catchman as he stepped into the alleyway, materializing from the shadows. The air seemed to drop in temperature.

He waited, still. I could faintly hear his breathing, so quiet I could barely distinguish it over the tiny breeze. And once again, like last night, I went cold with fear, as if my body had suddenly lost all power to keep out the night chill, and it was soaking into me like water into a sponge.

The Catchman? Here again? *What did he want with us?*

110

Then he began to come up the alley. His footsteps were feather-soft; his body stayed crouched low to the ground, insidious. He was moving slowly, stopping every few steps to listen, but always advancing.

If he catches me out here, I'm dead, I thought. *But if I let him get inside Mos Eisley, he'll kill again. And this time it could be Skeet or Leanne.*

Then a thought struck me, and I clenched my fist in frustration and horror as I realized what I'd done. I'd left the back door unlocked, on the latch, so I could get back in when I was done wandering. The Catchman could just walk in there.

What was I gonna do? I chewed my lip, my eyes flitting around as if inspiration could he found in the dark corners of my neighbour's yard. Silently, I slid my butterfly knife out and unfolded the blade from its guard. I felt a little better with the cold metal of the handle in my grip, but not much. I remembered how useless it had been last time.

Another few steps, and then a pause. He was careful, so careful. Maybe that's why he hadn't been caught yet. The muscles of my forearm were tensed, my hand clasped tight on my knife. Any second now, it was time to make the choice. Fight, or let him pass.

I already knew the answer to that. I couldn't let him in. Not with Leanne and Skeet in there.

But the thought of coming face-to-face with that blank hood filled me with terror, and the thought of what I might see *beneath* that hood was even worse.

Another set of shuffling footsteps. He was almost at our back yard now. I could see him, in my mind's eye, his hood swinging this way and that, searching. Searching for *me*.

Do it!

But I couldn't. I was paralysed. The thought of meeting him again, after the effortless way he wasted me last time – I knew if I went up against him, I couldn't hope to win. But I had no other choice.

DO IT!

I gritted my teeth, knuckles whitening on the handle of my knife. I had to face him. I had to bring him down, before he got us all.

NOW!

And then a loud crash made me jump, down at the far end of the alleyway, accompanied by a terrific feline yowl. The cat had knocked something over – a plant pot off a wall or something. I heard the rustle of his habit as the Catchman whirled in alarm.

Reprieved! Seizing my chance, I leaped over the wall. I caught a fleeting glimpse of the black robes of the murderer as I sprinted across our tiny back yard, heading not for the Catchman, but for the back door. He swung back, springing for me; but I threw the door open, darted inside, and slammed it shut, clicking the latch home.

Breathless, I slid down beneath the window that looked out over our yard, my back to the door. Outside, there was silence. I waited for what seemed an age. Had he gone, frightened off? My ears strained to pick out a sound. Nothing.

After a time, I couldn't take not knowing any longer. I had to see. Was he still out there? Quietly, I turned myself around and gently rose to look out of the window.

He was there, centimetres from the glass, my own reflected face looking back at me from within the dark frame of his hood.

I yelled, my heart lurching like it had been kicked, falling away from the window and the figure that was there, looking in at me like the manifestation of Death. He just stood there, unmoving, invisible eyes staring at me. He was making no move to come in, just waiting, as if say: *You've got to open this door sometime, Davey. And when you do, I'll be here.*

Then . . . footsteps. Running steps from the alley-way outside – Fiver and Bannon. The Catchman paused, looked to the left, then to the right – and then he melted away from the window, returning to the shadows.

They found me on the floor, my knife held out in front of me, slashing at anyone who came near. It was a long time before they'd calmed me down enough to get any sense out of me.

12

I don't remember much of what happened after that. Leanne put me to bed, I think, and she looked after me for a little while until I fell asleep. I reckon it was around two-ish, but I can't be sure. Anyway, I was a bit of a wreck. I do remember thinking, though: *Thank God tonight's over and done.*

Wrong.

The next thing I knew was being shaken awake. A flat grey light was beginning to suffuse the room, the first stirrings of a new (and equally drab) winter day. My head was thumping, and at first I physically couldn't wake up; but eventually the persistent shaking got through to me and I finally groaned and opened my eyes a tiny bit.

"Whadd*you*wan'?" I mumbled, my face still pressed into the pillow, one eye staring accusingly at the shape of Win, kneeling by my bedside.

"Wake up, Davey," she whispered.

I raised myself up and rolled on to my side, my eyes still half-closed. Every time I blinked, my eyelids tried to droop themselves back together. "I'm awake," I said faintly.

"Come on, get up," she urged.

The way I was feeling, I couldn't muster the

strength to argue. I was still fully clothed except for my shoes, which Leanne had taken off for me, so I nudged aside my blankets (they seemed so *heavy*, suddenly) and arranged myself so I was sitting on the edge of my mattress.

"Talk fast," I said blearily. "You got thirty seconds to give me an out-*stan*-ding reason to stay awake or I hit the sack again."

"You gotta help me, Davey," she said. "Please!"

By now certain details were sifting back into my jellied brain, like what had happened to Dino tonight. And how messed up Win had been about it all.

"I need to get out of here, Davey, I can't do it without your help," she said. "Benjy's put people on the doors. I need you to distract 'em for me."

"Why?" I asked, being obtuse.

She knitted her fingers together anxiously. "I got a home to go to. I don't wanna stay here."

I looked at her, still trying to work her out.

"I can't stay in this house with *him* here!" she cried, her voice rising. "He's dead! I need my parents. I wanna be at home! Don't you get that?" Her voice dropped. "I've had enough of ghosts."

"You're not still on *that*, are you?" I sighed.

"I know how you guys make fun of me," she snapped, her face growing red. "I know you don't believe in 'em. But I *do*, okay? And I believe the Catchman is a ghost – and so do a lot of other people. Just read the papers!"

115

She waited for me to smirk or something, but I was too tired to bother.

"Think about it, Davey," she said, taking my non-reaction as a sign that I might be persuaded to join her loon-o side of the argument. "Whoever it was, they got in and out without any of us seeing them. Twice. And—"

"Win, *I* could get in and out of this place twice without anyone seeing me. Even Bannon probably could, if he didn't trip over his forehead. We aren't security guards. We're disorganized, we're lazy, and we can't work together on anything. Even a complete stranger could get in and out like that if they watched the house for a while."

"But you're forgetting one thing," Win said, in a tone that suggested she thought she was Columbo or Poirot or something. "This all started when you tagged that cross in the graveyard. Y'know, graveyards . . . crosses . . . any of this sound likely?"

"No," I said. "It sounds like the plot of a bad horror movie."

"Oh, whatever. Will you help me get out or not?" she demanded, pooching out her lower lip.

I didn't have much sympathy for her situation, not like I'd done with Leanne when she'd heard about Rob Alder's death. Win was a daft bint who'd been a pain ever since I came to Mos Eisley. But I agreed anyway. Maybe I was just doing it to get on Benjy's nerves. Or maybe it was 'cause I didn't have anything

116

better to do, except sleep, and I could hardly do that with this walrus lowing in my ear.

"Okay then," I said, slipping my shoes on. "Who's on which door?"

"Fiver's on the back, Benjy's out front."

"Back door, then."

"'Kay," she said, smiling now that I was helping her.

I sighed as I got up, making it clear what a chore it was to do this. "You know Benjy'll never let you back once you're gone."

"I know," she said. "Thanks, Davey." Then, impulsively, she hugged me. I shoved her violently off me. She looked at me like I'd stabbed her.

"I don't like to be touched," I said. Well, not by her, anyway.

"Sorry," she said, looking like a kicked puppy.

I got up and led the way out of my room. Nobody would be upstairs; everybody had been conscripted for Benjy's stupid patrol. But we stopped on the balcony, watching the hall. After a few moments, Bannon and Skeet sloped by, both looking unhappy at being stationed with the other, both knackered out of their minds.

After they were gone, we slipped down into the hall, and into the back corridor that led past Leanne and Benjy's door. Benjy was probably a touch disgruntled at having to take my place on the patrol; bless him, like I *care*. Then I saw the back door, and for a moment my eyes went wide as I imagined the hooded

117

face of the Catchman in the window, looking in at me.

"Come *on*!" Win said, pulling my arm.

I snapped out of it, looking round at her and then at the back door again. There was nothing there, only the sight of our back yard gradually taking on the light of a reluctant dawn.

"Wait here," I said. "As soon as you see him leave, get out." Then I went through.

Fiver was sitting outside, on the same wall I'd been hiding behind a few hours before. As I came through the door, he jerked awake; he'd nodded into a semi-doze.

"Alright, Fiver?" I said.

"Tired," he replied, giving me a fragile smile.

"Yeah, me as well."

"This whole thing sucks worse than anything."

"Yeah," I agreed.

He looked at me cautiously. I think he was still way disturbed over what had happened to Dino, and the state I'd been in earlier.

'What happened to you out here?" he asked.

"I don't need to tell you. You already know."

"It *was* him?"

I nodded, one of my dreads falling over my face as I did. I brushed it back.

"Listen, you wanna get some sleep?"

Fiver's dulled eyes lit up.

"I'll cover the post. Can't sleep anyway."

"Really?"

"No problem."

"Thanks," he said.

"Go round the front and tell Benjy what I said. He'll only blow his top if you don't."

"Okay, sure," he said, and scampered off to comply.

I ushered Win through. She came warily into the back yard.

"Go on," I said.

She looked at me with fawning gratitude in her eyes. It made me a little sick. Realizing I would probably never see her again, I suppose I should have said something a little more heartfelt than what came next. Still. . .

"Get lost," I told her.

It was more a reaction to the disgust I felt at her look than any truly deep emotion; but her face fell, and without a word she turned and ran for freedom. Did I say *freedom*? Yeah, I s'pose that's right. It was dumb, but we were virtually prisoners in Mos Eisley, trapped here because, for most of us, it was our only home and if we deserted Benjy now, he'd never let us back in. And I, of course, was trapped by Leanne.

A moment after Win had disappeared, Fiver came back. "He's not out there," he said briefly, confusion on his face.

"Benjy?"

"He's not at his post."

"Let's find him, then," I said. "Get the others."

*

I gotta confess, we could have been more organized. Instead, grateful that our jailor had gone for a while and that we had an excuse to leave Mos Eisley, everybody dispersed to search the streets. Obviously, we had the sense to check the house first. I woke Leanne, who was understandably alarmed. The bruise on her cheek was fading fast, but the sight of it still made me think twice about what I would do if I found Benjy alone.

It was about this time that Win's absence was noticed, as well. Her car was gone from where it was usually parked. Bannon gave me a knowing look, as if the fact that she had gone proved she had murdered Dino. Everybody else was panicked that she had disappeared along with Benjy. I pretended not to know anything. Let 'em think what they want.

Anyway, after all the pointless discussion was brought to a close, we split up and the dawn search began. Skeet suggested going in pairs in case the Catchman was still around, and then said he'd go with Fiver. It was a surprise move on his part, but he knew what he was doing. No way would Leanne go with Bannon; she was left to go with me. I can't say I was that unhappy about it. Bannon was the odd one out, but he said he didn't mind going on his own. And if any of us could fight off the Catchman, it was gonna be him.

We set off through the brightening streets. I say *brightening* in a relative way, as no amount of sunshine could make these streets anything but gloomy. Even when it was midsummer, instead of being pleasant they took on a dusty, blasted air, the heat trapped by pollution.

Leanne was fretting it badly; she knew Benjy wouldn't ever abandon his post like that, not when he'd been such a tyrant about it with everybody else. He was a stubborn, jealous mook, but he wasn't a hypocrite, and at least he practised what he preached. It made me feel vaguely annoyed that she wasted so much affection on him after everything he had done to her, but that was the way she was.

We'd taken a roundabout route, me leading, wandering the streets in search of Benjy. We had skipped off the main road across some scrubby waste land when I became conscious of Leanne beginning to slow down. Even before I saw what was up ahead, I knew what she had seen.

From a patch of thistle and gorse that grew amid the mounds of hard earth, we could see the tip of a boot sticking out. And just from those few centimetres of dirty black toecap, I knew that whoever it belonged to had not tripped and fallen, was not just unconscious or even just blind drunk. He or she was dead.

Leanne looked away, and even I began to feel a little queasy. It wasn't the thought of the body, it was just – I mean, *another* one? This wasn't just a one-off, this was a massacre! The Catchman was killing, and killing, too much and too fast and too many. It was like—

I stopped myself. First we see who it is. Leanne stayed where she was while I walked slowly over to the body. The scuffing of my feet sounded unnaturally loud, even against the faint morning chorus of the birds that greeted the dawn. Tiny clouds of dirt billowed up from my soles. My eyes were fixed on the body, as my progress nearer gradually removed the obstruction, of the wild patch of thistle and weeds.

My heart sank. I saw who it was. I saw the strangle-marks. How was I gonna tell Leanne this? She was upset enough already.

Stony-faced, I walked back to her. One hand was in my hair, anxiously scratching the side of my skull through the matted hair at the base of my dreads.

She was looking at me, anxiety and fear and the anticipation of bad news in her dark eyes. "Who *is* it?"

I opened my mouth to speak, and shut it again. I wanted to make it easy on her, tell her as softly as I could, but the words just weren't coming into my head.

"Who *is* it?" she asked again, her voice rising in pitch. "Is it Benjy? *Is* it?"

My shoulders sagged, and I let out a sigh.

"It's Win," I said. "The Catchman got her."

13

"Where *were* you?" I exploded, shoving Benjy on the shoulders. "You give us all this about staying put, about guarding the house, and then you just *go off*? For all we know, *you* could have done Win over!"

There was a sudden silence as I said that. Me and Benjy were facing up. I was mad, but I shouldn't have said that. I shouldn't have let him know that I suspected him.

When we'd got back from the search, Leanne was in a pretty bad state. But what was worse, Benjy just sauntered in a few minutes later like nothing was wrong, and then called everyone stupid for worrying about him. The news about Win, however, had apparently been a surprise to him; and he'd darkened with rage when I told him.

"We know who did it," Benjy said. He'd adopted the challenging tone that me and him seemed to be trading more and more often of late. "It doesn't matter that I wasn't here."

"We *know*?" I echoed scornfully. "You're not gonna tell me you think it was Jamie Archer as well?"

"Course it was Jamie Archer!" he exploded. "Who else *could* it have been?"

"It could have been *anyone*," I cried. "The Catchman could be anyone. Why does it have to be him? You seriously think he's capable of killing *two* of us as payback for Rob? He's not a *gangster*. He's just a kid, like us!"

"He thinks we killed Rob Alder," Benjy insisted, "and this is his way of getting back at us."

"It isn't him!"

"And you'd know this, huh?" Benjy said. "No you wouldn't. None of us know what Jamie's capable of. Not till now, anyway."

I covered my face with my hand. I was fighting a losing battle. The lynch-mob majority was firmly in effect here. And that meant that the most obvious solution was the one that was right. No, maybe that's a dumb analogy. I mean, nobody except Bannon and Benjy wanted a *fight*, exactly. But I could tell that they were all either too scared, too tired or too stupid to argue with Benjy's logic right now, and no amount of persuading on my part would change their minds.

"Are you with me or not?" Benjy said eventually, breaking the silent deadlock. "'Cause if you're not, just turn around and get outta here, know what I mean? Don't come back."

Out of the corner of my eye I saw Skeet look up. I knew what he was thinking. He wanted to get gone; this just wasn't fun any more. And I was tempted then – so tempted, right on the verge of telling Benjy where to go and leaving Mos Eisley and all this behind. But then I remembered Leanne, saying: *Don't go. I want you to stay.*

124

"Alright," I said grudgingly. Benjy had played his strongest hand, forcing me to either back him or leave. But I couldn't leave Mos Eisley yet; I still had things to do. I had to win Leanne over completely before it fell apart. But everybody could see that Benjy's attempts to pin it on his arch-enemy were getting increasingly desperate. Now it just seemed as if he were spoiling for a fight, and wanted us to back him up.

I thought I'd play along for now. Everything he did made him look more and more out of control. And I could tell the others were thinking the same thing, Leanne included. He was getting unhinged. They were getting wary of him.

I heard Skeet tut in disgust at my acquiescence. He was reaching the end of his tether perilously fast. Even a docile goofball like Skeet had his limits, and I was testing them a little too much. By agreeing to go with Benjy, I'd virtually forced him to do it as well, because he wouldn't leave without me, just like I wouldn't leave without Leanne.

I know I'm selfish, but that doesn't stop me feeling bad about it when I am.

I looked up at Benjy then, a sudden thought occurring. "You never did tell me where you went."

Benjy gazed back coolly. "I was getting rid of Dino's body," he said.

We went into Abbey Cross. This time we did it *my* way, taking a roundabout, back-street route through the arteries of the city to make sure that we weren't seen. Leanne had been left behind, alone, at the house, a situation I wasn't very happy about; but at least Benjy was here, where I could see him.

With me and Benjy were Fiver, Skeet and Bannon. Benjy walked alone at the front, striding angrily, pretending to be oblivious to the looks we were giving him and the whispers that passed between us.

He had *got rid* of Dino's body?

The story went that he had dragged him from the ground-floor bedroom and put him in the boot of Win's car. The poor, misguided dink kept a spare set of keys on one of those magnetic key clamps under the wheel-arch. Like *that's* not the most obvious place to look. Anyway, Benjy knew about it somehow, so he took the body to the river and dumped it. He told us he did it on his own 'cause he knew we'd be squeamish about it.

I didn't have to point out that, because he'd taken Win's car, she'd had to walk home. And that was why she'd been strangled.

Nobody had argued with him. I don't think anyone knew where to *start*. The enormity of what had been done had struck us all dumb. Nobody asked him why he'd done it, either. Maybe he didn't want his fragile dream of Mos Eisley to be shattered by the police; maybe he didn't want us all to split up and disappear, torn apart by the killings. I don't know.

And maybe he got rid of the body 'cause he didn't

want to be caught. Maybe he *was* the killer. He was afraid that the cops would link him and Rob Alder if they found a body in Mos Eisley. Anyway, whether it was true or not, that was what everyone thought. I could tell by the looks they were giving him. They were scared of him.

Oh Benjy, I thought with a bitter inward smile, *you ain't guilty, but you're doing such a good job of making yourself look it. And you can't even see it. You're letting yourself get swept up in the Catchman's legend. That's why you're not thinking straight – none of us are. That's why you have to lash out at someone. It's got us all by the throat as surely as if it was the Catchman himself, and we're all just running in circles, snapping at our own tails.*

I shook myself back to the task at hand. It'd taken me some time to persuade Benjy that we couldn't just plough in there and not expect to get beaten senseless; after all, we were only five now, and Fiver and Skeet hardly counted. So if he was gonna go through with this plan, we had to get Jamie Archer on his own.

Our task was made unexpectedly easier by Fiver, who informed us in an offhand sort of way that Jamie worked in a chippy for three days of the week, and this was one of those days.

Following this particular bombshell, we made our plans. Personally, I didn't have a lot of enthusiasm for it, but – well, I did still owe him for clubbing me the day before last. My conscience gave me a sorta cursory nudge, just to let me know it had made a protest, then disappeared entirely. I think my conscience wanted to see him battered just as much as the rest of me.

We all knew where the chippy was; it was on one of the roads that ran just off the main street. The trick was to get Jamie.

Thanks mainly to my incomparable navigation, we got through the grim streets and alleys of Abbey Cross without being seen by any of Jamie's lot. Sour-faced pensioners and grubby kids in tracksuits who were skiving even at their young age watched us pass. We came up on a gravel drive which ran along the side of the little row of shops that the chippy belonged to; and after sending Fiver around the front to check Jamie was actually working there today, we climbed over the high wooden gate that led into the small back yard of the chippy.

The yard was a small patch of concrete to park cars in. There were no cars there today. Apart from a couple of steamed-up, meshed-over windows, the only other feature in the blank wall that faced us was a small door that couldn't be opened from the outside without a key.

Because of the high wall and gate, we couldn't be seen from the gravel drive. We took up position around the door, and waited.

Fiver returned a moment later, hitching over the top of the gate and dropping down the other side.

"He's the only one working today," he said, glancing nervously at us. Fiver didn't like violence much. He always maintained he preferred anonymous, victimless crime where nobody got hurt except people who had enough money not to care. But in this situation, and in Benjy's mind, violence was the only option.

The back room was where they kept all the frozen sacks of chips. We knew it was only a matter of time before he ran out of chips in the fryers, and came back to get some more. That was when we'd do it.

Thankfully, Jamie chose to cooperate sooner than we thought. I don't think I could have hacked it for long, standing there in silence with everybody glancing at each other. We were all in sorta delayed shock or something about Dino, but things had happened so fast that nobody had had time to deal with it, so everyone had shovelled it under the carpet for later. It made for some bad feeling between us. Everything was pretty strained.

Anyway, it couldn't have been more than two minutes before we heard the loud rustle of frozen chips being dragged out, and saw Jamie's shape moving about inside. Benjy knocked on the door.

I saw him pause and look up, completely unaware of what was waiting for him. Then he came over. We heard the latch turn and he pulled the door open.

Mistake.

I can still remember the look of surprise in his eyes

as Benjy grabbed the front of his shirt with two fists and yanked him out into the yard. He was completely off-balance, his hands flailing the air as he stumbled forward and fell to the concrete floor on his hands and knees. Fiver reached through and shut the door behind him, cutting off his escape route. And then we all piled into him.

I gotta admit, I didn't kick him as hard as I could have. I was pulling the force out of my swings to some extent, because I wasn't really wholeheartedly into this. I didn't hate Jamie Archer, not like Benjy did. But it didn't matter; I still laid into him with the rest of them, running with the pack.

At first he tried to crawl away from us so he could get to his feet; but this just left his legs and stomach exposed, and we swung kicks and rabbit-punches into them. I don't think he once raised his head to see who was doing it; if he had, he'd probably have got the sole of someone's combats in it anyway. Besides, he knew just who it was who was threading him.

I'll give him credit, though; he stood up to it for longer than I've ever seen anyone do. It took a whole load of battery before he finally curled up into the protective foetal position that I've seen so many times, his arms wrapped around his head, and just lay there and took it.

I thought I was the first to stop. At least, until I realized that Fiver had never really started; he'd just pretended to so as not to make Benjy mad. That kid is so touchingly pacifist. Skeet followed my lead, anyway. He'd had enough.

But Bannon and Benjy hadn't finished. They were still laying into Jamie, really putting their body weight behind their kicks. He jerked in response to the vicious blows they were dealing him. Us three who had stopped looked at each other, concern in our eyes.

Benjy's face was twisted in a snarl of absolute hatred and fury; his skin was almost purple. Bannon, who had a nasty disposition anyway, was doing it for the sheer enjoyment, but Benjy – I have *never* seen anyone or anything so insane with rage as he was.

"You like that?" he screamed as he laid the boot in. *"Murderer! You like it, huh? Here, have some more!"*

Well, that was it. He was firmly off his box, and I wasn't gonna stand by and let him cripple an innocent kid. I ran over to him, wrapping his arms behind him and pinning them there, dragging him back.

"Get off me!" he screamed. *"I'll kill you! Get off me!"*

Bannon gave up kicking Jamie now and backed away, looking confused. Without Benjy taking the lead, he was lost. But Benjy was writhing like a cobra in my grip, trying to throw me off.

"He's had enough! Leave him! He's—" I shouted in his ear, but I never got any further. He twisted suddenly, reversing my hold on him, and flung me over his shoulder on to the concrete. It knocked the breath from my body, but I managed to land it right, so

I only got a whacking great bruise instead of breaking my ribs.

But he'd lost interest in me. I saw the flash of a knife appearing in his hand. I tried to shout something, but no sound would come, and then he brought it down, driving it into Jamie's back.

That moment seemed to last for ever.

And then Jamie's scream of agony cut through the silence, and I saw Benjy pull the knife out for another stab. And I knew I couldn't do anything about it.

But a moment before he struck, he was barrelled off his feet by a figure that shoulder-charged him in the stomach and knocked him reeling. His knife flew from his hand, and he staggered back a step; a moment later, a boot flashed from nowhere, hammering between his legs.

I couldn't credit it. *Fiver*.

Benjy's howl was almost the equal of Jamie's. For a moment he was frozen in pain, and then he dropped to his knees and spewed all over the concrete floor. Bannon made a grab for Fiver, but the little kid was away, leaping up and over the wooden gate. Voices were beginning to call from inside the chippy, from concerned or impatient customers who would be coming to investigate any moment.

Then Skeet ran up to me, helping me to my feet.

"We're goin'," he said.

Together we ran past the prone form of Benjy and the bewildered slab of Bannon, and on my way, I scooped up Benjy's knife so he couldn't do any more harm with it. Then we followed Fiver's lead, over the wooden gate and into the winding back streets of Abbey Cross.

14

Me and Skeet went into town after that. I wanted to go back to Mos Eisley, just to have one last go at persuading Leanne to come with us, but Skeet wouldn't have any of it. He knew that'd be the first place Benjy and Bannon would head for, and he didn't want to meet them till they'd calmed down some.

So instead I dragged him to the movies to see those Drew Barrymore flicks they were re-running. I needed time to think and get my head together. I had to work out what I was gonna do next.

I don't think I've ever explained to you my Drew Barrymore fixation, have I? I dunno, just a childish thing that got out of hand. I mean, we even share the same birthday, 22nd February.

Course, she's about four years older than me, but in Hollywood terms, that's less than nothing. I still entertain hopes of going over to the big U S of A and stalking her for a while.

They were showing *Poison Ivy*, *Far From Home* and *No Place to Hide*, three fairly diabolical films made bearable only by the fact that Drew stars in them. I always liked her in her sorta sixteen-to-eighteen period, even though the films were terrible. After that, she must have fired her agent and got a new one or something, 'cause she started appearing in loads of romantic dramas, which are no doubt very good but which I've never had any desire to watch. The one exception was *Scream*, which definitely wasn't a romantic drama, but she was only in that for about ten minutes before being butchered in a reasonably distressing manner by a guy dressed in a spook mask. Tasty.

We sat there in the darkened auditorium munching pick'n'mix that had been bought with the money Skeet had nicked from the house pool. It had struck me as a little weird how the pool always seemed to be a little low on certain days of the week; turns out Skeet had been slyly embezzling himself a bit of an emergency fund for situations just like this. I hardly had any cause to complain; it was all Fiver's money, anyway.

All three films I knew well enough to recite the script backwards, and I kept on falling asleep in the dark, 'cause I'd had a rough few nights and was fairly well knackered. Anyway, the point was, I wasn't really paying much attention in the cinema; my thoughts were on other things.

Fiver, to start with. He'd never dare come back and we all knew it. The linchpin of our gang was gone for ever. And without him and his money, the whole lot was gonna crumble. Nothing could stop that now.

It was always gonna happen, really, right from the start. My attempts to split up the Park Estate gang were only hastening the inevitable. Recently, though, I'd excelled myself. Benjy had been getting more and more unbalanced and erratic. Now he'd completely lost the plot. What was he thinking, anyway? I mean, dumping Dino's body in a river? And he was actually gonna *kill* Jamie.

We were all in real bad trouble.

Oh yeah, and I vaguely wondered whether Jamie Archer was still alive, and how much it would add to my jail sentence if he wasn't.

The films finished, we left the cinema and hit the arcades. We were sitting next to each other in the driving chairs of a Sega Rally machine, racing head-to-head, when Skeet said: "That's it, then."

"What's it?" I asked, over the static of bleeps and video game music that fogged the arcade.

"The gang. The whole thing. S'over and done."

"Hang on," I said, slamming on the brakes and unwisely throwing the steering wheel to full lock. Predictably, I totalled my car, but a few moments later, it was back on the road, healthy and shiny, just in time to see Skeet race by me in his white Ford Escort or whatever it was.

"What I'm sayin' is," he continued, "we can leave it all behind now, right? There ain't any point goin' back to Mos Eisley. With Fiver gone, that's it. And all this stuff with the Catchman – it ain't worth it any more."

He looked over, at me. "If you go back there, I ain't coming with you. I'm gone."

I negotiated a particularly tricky chicane while I gave him my reply: "I *am* going back there. But only once. Just to get her. Give her a final choice: him or me. That fair?"

"S'pose so," he said sulkily.

"After that, we're gone, okay? No more Mos Eisley. Greener pastures and all that stuff. You with me?" I really meant it, too: I was sick of the whole thing now, sick and scared. I was afraid to spend another night in Mos Eisley. I'd given Leanne enough chances and I'd stretched my friendship with Skeet far enough. When it came down to it, it had always been me and him; and if it got to the wire, I'd never leave my best mate.

Besides, I thought slyly as he grunted an affirmative, I can always come back later for Leanne.

We both drove for a bit; I was taking reckless risks to catch up with him, and it was just making me crash more and fall farther behind.

"What we gonna do if Jamie's dead?" he said.

"Same thing we're gonna do anyway," I said. "Look, it don't really matter if he's dead or not; police'll still be after us. We still had a hand in it. So we leave. Go to a different city. Disappear. It ain't hard; we've been practically invisible for a year now anyway."

"Okay," he said; then we both looked at each other and chorused: "Got nothing better to do."

I looked back at the screen. I'd committed myself

now. Maybe it was better that way. I mean, Skeet was right and I knew it. This whole Leanne thing was stupid. She'd had chance after chance to leave with me, but instead she stayed with a guy who knocked her around and treated her like dirt. Mmm, *interesting* use of logic there, Leanne.

Anyway, I'd freely admit to being pretty taken with her, but I wasn't gonna go to jail for her. And that's what'd happen if I stuck around for much longer. After what had happened to Jamie – well, let's say the sand in our hourglass had suddenly started falling a whole lot faster.

So there it was. One more chance, and then I was blowing this place with Skeet.

I'd really have to make this one *count*.

We spent a little time messing about in town. Neither of us wanted to go back to Mos Eisley until Benjy had cooled down a bit, so we just faffed around like we'd done all our lives. It wasn't a hard thing to do. We were born to be slack, and we could loaf weeks away if we weren't careful. While we were hanging out, we worked out what we were gonna say to Benjy when we got back. Skeet came up with the idea of telling him we went after Fiver, trying to catch him and kick him in for what he'd done to Benjy. I loved it – dishonest *and* hypocritical. I'd probably have shaken Fiver's hand if I met him again. Like I said before, I was sorta fond of the kid. I hoped he was alright, wherever he was.

After a while Skeet said he wanted to go back, but I didn't feel up to it yet. I needed a bit of time alone to work out my plan, my last stab at getting Leanne. I said I'd see him later. He told me to be careful. I said I would.

15

Being winter, it got dark early. It wasn't long after Skeet had left that full night descended on the city and the streetlights flickered on. It was unseasonably warm tonight, which was a bonus as I was sick of freezing to death every time the sun went down.

I walked, trolling along at my usual pace, taking a long and winding route back towards Mos Eisley. I needed the space, time to think up a strategy for Leanne. I let my feet take me on automatic. I ambled around for maybe an hour before I hit on something which stopped me in my tracks. I leaned against a wall, working it all out in my head, weighing up the pros and cons – and then a smile crept across my face.

A moment later, I was heading for home. I was quite a way out from the Park estate, so I took the back roads and little-used routes through the city that I knew so well. I reckoned I'd been walking for only about ten or fifteen minutes before I pulled up abruptly.

I blinked. I knew where I was, of course – just by the municipal car park. There was a shortcut that went between two streets, a path that ran past Tesco and a parking bay, presumably for trucks that were unloading into the supermarket. Up ahead was the towering bulk of the MCP, and just in front of me was the pedestrian tunnel that ran through to the street opposite, and another, smaller short-stay car park beyond.

Usually, the tunnel had little lozenge-shaped lights along the ceiling to light the way at night. Today, there was only a heavy blackness inside.

I hesitated. The path ran along the left side of the wall; on the right side there was a railing, and beyond that the curving down-ramp for the cars to get out. Even without the light it was easy enough to follow the railing to the other side, and I could see the dim square of moonglow at the far end. Maybe it was 'cause I was jittery anyway, or maybe intuition, but something was telling me: *Don't go in there, you idiot!*

But what else was I gonna do? Turn around and go back? That'd put me at least five minutes out of my way, an effort that could be easily saved by travelling through fifteen metres of darkness – a journey that wouldn't take me more than thirty seconds. By now I was getting a little footsore (I'd been on my feet all day), and I was beginning to think that Mos Eisley might not be such a bad place after all.

But he's in *there*, came the voice again. It didn't take me long to figure out who *he* was.

How could he be? I thought to myself. You're just getting spooked, 'cause of all the stuff that happened last night. Don't be a mook.

I stood there for a few moments, marshalling my

courage. Then I took a breath, refusing to be intimidated, and plunged into the darkness of the pedestrian tunnel.

The sounds of the night seemed to just drop dead as soon as I stepped inside, to be replaced by the pregnant silence of the concrete. My boots thudded slowly beneath me, a dull rhythm that seemed to be swallowed up by the hungry dark. I was forcing myself to keep my steps slow, but something inside me was climbing my spine, wrapping tight fingers around my lungs, making me short of breath. I was afraid, like I had been that first night when I thought I'd heard the Catchman but it had turned out to be Benjy.

I stopped. Listened. Had that been...? Nah. Imagination. The downside of having such a volatile imagination is that you can create yourself some preetty interesting nightm—

There it was *again*. A noise, sibilant and faint, as if someone had dropped a tin dustbin lid in the very far distance. But it didn't *sound* distant. It was coming from the dark abyss on the other side of the railing to my right, from the car ramp.

I resumed walking, but my hand had slipped into my pocket, clutching the folded rectangle of my butterfly knife. If I ran, I could make it easily to the other side of the tunnel and be out – but I wasn't *going* to run. Because this was all in my head, right? I gritted my teeth. It was getting to be a sloppy state of affairs when you couldn't even trust your own senses any more.

"*Daaaveeey*," came a voice, so faint it was difficult to hear. But it wasn't the word that froze me, it was who was saying it. My dad! It was my dad's voice!

"It's not *you*!" I cried, my voice frighteningly loud in comparison. "You're *dead*!"

"*Stop walking, Davey,*" breathed the darkness. "*Can't you wait for your old dad?*"

But I carried on going, refusing to run, keeping my pace steady even though my legs trembled, not turning around to look.

"You're in my head, Dad. You're not here. I saw you. I saw you dead."

"*But I* am *here, Davey. I'm always with you. And I'm going to stay with you until you stop kidding yourself. Until you stop trying to deny what you are. Won't you stop and listen?*"

"No," I hissed through clenched teeth.

"*You're me, Davey. And I'm you. Like father—*"

"Like son," I finished, my voice shaking a little. "No. *No!* You're *not* here, and *I'm* not crazy. Whoever's out there, if I find you, you're *dead*."

"*I'm right here, Davey. Why don't you come in and find me?*"

"Yeah," I said to myself, my teeth gritted in anger to combat the fear that had swelled inside. "I might just do that." And with that, I vaulted the rail on the side of the walkway and stepped into the darkness of the car ramp.

The voice fell silent, and I stopped still, listening.

Yeah, that called your bluff, didn't it? With my blade in my hand, whoever was messing with me wasn't quite so confident.

My eyes had adjusted to the darkness enough so that I could see the vague outlines of the stone edges of the ramp; but the blackness around still attacked me on some kind of primal level, worrying at me with the fear that I couldn't see far enough around me to protect myself from danger. Whoever it was –

you know who it is

– who was in here, they'd be –

But what if there's nobody in here? What if it really is all in your head?

I made a mental effort to shut up the insistent voice in my mind, the one that had been questioning and bugging me all day. It was getting on my nerves, and right now I needed my wits about me.

In the abyss of darkness, the faint chiming-crashing noise came again. From above me, I thought. Slowly, moving my feet carefully in case there was anything I might trip on, I began to move through the emptiness, heading up the ramp. It was tortuously slow going, but every second, my eyes were adjusting more and more to the feeble light, and now I could make out a little more detail.

"Come on, then!" I shouted scornfully. "Where are you now, *Dad*?"

There was no reply. If anything, the silence was worse than that awful, insidious voice. Silently, semi-blind, I moved onward, heading slowly up the concrete incline of the ramp. At the top of the next level, I looked back to where the pedestrian tunnel was; it seemed impossibly distant, the moonlight providing the only visual anchor in the nightmarish darkness of the MCP.

You idiot! Turn back! came that voice again, the one I'd been trying to suppress. Its tone was different – still as negative as ever, but now really scared, with an edge of panic to it. *What are you trying to prove?*

"I'm gonna prove that I'm not nuts," I said under my breath. "I'm not hearing my dad in my head, I'm hearing him because someone's *imitating* him. And I'm gonna find out who."

You're not nuts? Then why are you talking to me? And why are you going blind into this place to prove yourself right? 'Cause if you are right, then you know who it is that'll be waiting for you.

"Yeah," I whispered. "I know."

There was a sound now, my ears homing in on it. It had got gradually louder as I had gone up the ramp, and even though it was close to being completely inaudible at the moment, once I had it pinned down it became terrifyingly loud.

Breathing.

I stopped. In among the vaguely bluish outlines that I could make out, there was no sign of anyone. But I could hear where it was coming from. I could hear it.

Where the car ramp looped around and went up again, there was a low wall to separate off the small pavement bit for pedestrians. It was coming from behind there. That was where he was waiting for me.

I tried to swallow, but my throat had clogged with phlegm and felt dry and sticky. Step after faltering step, I moved closer.

If I can't see him, he can't see me, I thought, trying to reassure myself, trying to quell the senses that were screaming at me to run for the light and safety of outdoors.

You don't sound very sure, came that voice again, the snide, nasty one in my head.

I gripped the handle of my knife. *I'm sure of* this *little baby, though*, I replied mentally, and that shut the voice up for now.

The low wall neared. The breathing became louder. Slow, raspy. Could he see me? Was I walking right into his hands? Cold sweat chilled my forehead, beads creeping between my dreads like insects.

And then the breathing stopped. And I heard the rustle of cloth behind me, the sound of the Catchman's habit as he leaped out of the darkness. I cried out, turning and falling backwards, my blade spinning out of my grip. I couldn't *see* him. *I couldn't see him.*

The next second, a blast of light dazzled me, and I instinctively threw my arm up in front of my eyes. Scrabbling away, I tried to see where my attacker was, where he'd—

I blinked. The lights in the car park had come back on. Whatever it had been (power cut?) that had killed the lights had been fixed.

But there was nobody here. No one. Nothing, except the flapping of a battered old paperback, which was caught in a breeze in the corner of one of the parking bays. I had no idea how it might have got there; its presence seemed almost surreal. Had the stirring of the pages been the breathing I had heard?

Acting on a compulsion I didn't understand, I picked up the book and opened it at random. I flicked to another page. Then another. Faster and faster, I turned the leaves, whipping them past beneath my fingers, and finally with a cry I threw the book down in the aisle and backed away from it, looking at it as if it was covered with blood.

It might as well have been. Every word, every single word in the book was the same phrase, over and over, end to end. . .

You are me.

Shaking my head in denial of what I was seeing, I took a step back and looked around the old concrete car park, as if searching for a way out of this horror.

My heart shuddered brutally against my ribcage.

The Catchman was standing at the bottom of the car ramp, his ragged, hunched form buried under dirty black robes.

This isn't happening! Not here!

And a moment later he was gone, flowing away,

disappearing from sight, leaving me unsure whether I'd ever seen him at all.

I waited, frozen, listening for a sound, watching for a movement – *anything*. But he was gone. His presence had departed. He could have taken me out now, easy as anything, but he didn't. He was playing with me.

I was beginning to tremble.

16

I walked back through the dark streets, setting a fast pace. Half of me wanted to run, but the other half told me not to. Running would just draw attention, and it wasn't as if I didn't look distinctive enough anyway, with my dreads and combats and all. If the police were looking for any of our gang – as I was sure they would be by now – then I didn't want to get collared before I managed to get out of the city.

I was shaken up badly after what had just happened to me. What – *who* was the Catchman? And even if I knew that, how did it explain all that stuff with the book? And what about that girl, the girl who I thought looked like Drew Barrymore, and what she'd said to me? And the hospital and the car park, when I thought I'd seen him but – but wasn't *sure*?

I was scared, scared and confused. I didn't know what to believe any more. Was the Catchman *really* what the legends made him out to be? Could he really appear and disappear at will? Could he *do* those things to me – mess with my mind like that, make me doubt even my own senses?

My pace slowed as I got back to the streets around Mos Eisley. I was especially wary now; it seemed like my enemies could be anywhere; whether they were Abbey Cross or Her Majesty's Constabulary – or worse. I never stopped glancing around as I walked through the yellow wash of the streetlights, until finally I got to Mos Eisley, going round the back way to avoid being seen.

I checked in the windows before I knocked on the door, but there was nothing I could see that provided a clue as to who was home. My heart was thudding just a little too hard as I rapped on the door. I dreaded what I might find inside, if nobody opened the door and I had to force it. Leanne dead? All of them, arranged like puppets around the floor of the living room?

The door opened. It was Leanne.

"Davey! Where've you been?" she asked, smiling through the worry on her face.

"Is that him?" called Benjy's voice irately from the living room.

"Come in," she said, hurrying me inside.

I walked into the living room, where Benjy, Skeet and Bannon were sitting by a fire. The change in the atmosphere was noticeable already. Mos Eisley no longer seemed like a home any more, just a dump of a house. The strange, tentative camaraderie that existed only a few days before had dissolved completely. Somehow, the place seemed bleaker, full of the knowledge that the last days of our gang had arrived. We'd all known that it couldn't last for ever; but now the end was here, I felt a little guilty. After all, the whole thing was partly my fault for feeding anybody's suspicions about Benjy. But it was always gonna happen, eventually. This gang was made to crumble with a leader like him.

"Where'd you go?" Benjy demanded, customarily polite.

I spun him our little story about chasing after Fiver; naturally, as we'd made it up together, it jibed with Skeet's version of events. He swallowed it hook, line, sinker, rod and fisherman. Once satisfied that we hadn't skanked him (which was another thing we intended to do ASAP), he proceeded to tell us his story about what had happened after we left. I won't bore you with the details, 'cause he was blatantly making most of it up, but the gist was that he and Bannon managed to get away before being seen, and had a couple of close shaves in Abbey Cross on the way back.

After he had finished, I asked, "D'you know if Jamie's still alive?"

"Do I care?" he returned.

"It's the difference between assault with a deadly weapon and murder; I think you *should* care."

"It was the Catchman I got," Benjy said, his blocky face animated. "They'll probably give me a medal."

I looked at the floor and scratched the back of my neck. I don't think he even knew what he'd done. I don't reckon any of it had really sunk in. Me and Skeet could disappear, maybe Bannon too. But Benjy – he wasn't like us. He'd hardly been outside the city, and he still relied on the charity of his parents far too much to make it in the real world. He couldn't run away from what he'd done. He was gonna go down, one way or another.

"You really think he was the Catchman?" I asked.

Benjy's eyes suddenly went cold, and I realized he was still dangerously on edge. "You saying he wasn't?" he said.

"I'm saying I saw the Catchman today," I replied levelly. I heard Leanne suck in her breath over her teeth behind me. "This evening. *After* you'd stuck Jamie."

The room seemed to darken even further. I looked at Benjy's face, demonic in the firelight, and I waited for him to say something.

"You're lying," he said eventually.

I laughed; couldn't help myself. "Good answer," I said sarcastically.

"You thought it was me, didn't you?" he said.

That stopped me laughing. I looked accusingly at Leanne.

"Yeah, she told me," he said. "You two might be *ever* so close, but I'm still her boyfriend."

I didn't take my eyes off her. She tried to glare back defiantly, but ended up averting her gaze. That *really* got me, what she had done. She'd been all confiding with me one minute, but as soon as she was alone with Benjy she couldn't help telling him. I'd have thought I would have learned by now, but no.

152

"Did she also tell you that *she* thought it was you as well?" I said.

Leanne looked at me in horror like I'd just slapped her, then at Benjy. Ah, so she hadn't told him *that* bit, I thought cruelly. Whether or not she'd meant it she *had* said it. She started to try and deny what she'd done, but Benjy's expression told her it was useless. Now pinned by both our gazes, she crumbled and ran out of the room.

I knew what I'd done; the minute they were alone again, Benjy was gonna batter her. I hadn't really thought about what I'd been doing – I just wanted to hit back at her. But strangely, it was probably the best thing I could have said; if I was gonna get her away from Benjy, the best way was to make her scared of him.

"Skeet, keep an eye on her," I said. He knew what I meant; I didn't want her left alone. He went to do as I told him. I turned back to Benjy. "The Catchman, it wasn't Jamie. You stabbed an innocent guy, like I *told* you in the first place. But you're too caught up being king of the castle to listen to anyone who talks any *sense*, aren't you?"

Benjy sneered. "You know what? I don't care. What you think don't make the slightest bit of difference to me."

"It doesn't matter anyway. It's not you. I know that." Now that Skeet and Leanne were out of the room, I could say that. Bannon didn't count; I wasn't bothered what he believed. "It was just a dumb suspicion."

"I'm *so* glad you've decided I'm innocent, Judge Davey," came the snide reply to my statement. "So now what are you gonna do?"

"I'm gonna finish this," I said. And I meant it. I was scared, and I didn't like feeling scared. It made me angry.

"How's that?" Bannon asked from the shadows, perking up.

"We need to go back to Abbey Cross cemetery, where all this started."

"Since when did you take charge here?" Benjy replied.

"Since now," I said, with a voice like a sabre. "I'm going anyway, with or without you. And anyone else who wants to come with me. But think about this: it's not gonna take long for the Abbey Cross boys to figure out who did over Jamie, and what d'you think they're gonna do when they work out it was us? And that's not even counting the police, who might have had witnesses who saw you running off and are on their way here now."

I saw Benjy and Bannon glance at each other as if they hadn't thought of that. Mooks. He looked back at me.

"You think anyone's gonna come with you?" he said. I don't think he had fully understood the challenge I had just made to his authority, but it was dawning on him pretty fast now. I could see the colour rising in his face.

"Do *you*?" I replied levelly. And he knew then what I meant. I saw realization dawn in his eyes. He'd let himself slip; nobody trusted him any more. By allowing himself to seem so guilty, by letting his stupid vendetta with Abbey Cross mess up all our lives, he'd lost everyone. He'd ostracized Fiver. He'd implicated us all in what could be a murder charge on Jamie, as if we didn't look guilty enough with dumping Dino's body. And Win's would soon be found as well. This was too much to just shovel under the carpet. This was the end. And what he knew, in that moment, was that he had brought about his own destruction.

I could tell he was struggling to digest it all.

"I ain't going anywhere till you tell me why you wanna go," he said at length, his voice weak, trying to salvage some pride out of the situation. He didn't *dare* go up against me on this. He knew he'd already lost. And he didn't want to take the risk that maybe, just maybe, *Leanne* might be on my side too.

'The Catchman's watching us somehow," I said. "I know he's around. How else could he have slipped past us to kill Dino, when Win had left for only a moment? And how else could he have followed Win and killed her? Even *you* can't say he doesn't exist now, with Jamie out of the picture." I paused. "I wanna go back to where it all started – Abbey Cross. If we stay here, he's gonna pick us off one by one. We need a battlefield. The cemetery."

"*What?*" Benjy cried, incredulous.

"If we go, he'll follow. He won't be able to resist."

"And you wanna *fight* him?"

"Sure," I said. "I've had enough. I wanna fight him. How about you? Better than sitting here and waiting to see who gets us first, the Catchman, the cops or Abbey Cross."

He looked at me hard, like he knew there was something more and he was trying to guess my intention. I expected him to be difficult. He surprised me.

"Okay. Alright. We all go," Benjy said, the words grating out between his teeth. He raised his voice. "*Even you, Leanne!*" Then he smirked at me. "I don't want her home alone if someone comes calling."

"Amen," I muttered under my breath, though my reasons were different from his.

"Let's get it together, everyone!" he shouted. "We've got ourselves a purpose, know what I mean?"

He was on his final command. He knew that I was only allowing him to pretend to be leader now. This would be the last charge of the Park Estate gang.

And the few of us who were left in Mos Eisley erupted in a flurry of preparation, darting through the black and peeling corridors to get ready to make one last trip into Abbey Cross.

17

I sorta had the feeling that this was where I came in, if you get me. Night, once again. Once more sneaking through the streets of Abbey Cross. The familiar flood of adrenalin. Me casting nervous glances over my shoulder at Benjy in case he was gonna put a pair of scissors in my back. (I'd pretended to lose his knife, though really I'd thrown it away into the river earlier in the day.)

There were important differences, though. This time, we wouldn't just suffer a pasting; if we were caught we'd be beaten within an inch of our lives. And if the estimate was off by an inch or so either way, well, none of 'em were gonna cry too hard about *that*.

Leanne was with us, too. And she was actually surprisingly good at this kinda stuff, using the shadows well. Still, we hadn't hit the real danger spots yet. We'd have to see how her nerve held up. I was sure she could hold her own, though.

She noticed me looking at her, and her eyes hardened. She was still sore about what I'd done to her. I shrugged to myself. She'd get over it once Benjy was gone. And the prospect of getting slapped around by a guy twice her weight had to count in my favour, even if it had never stopped her going back to him before.

The streets were quiet tonight; hardly anyone was around. Even the air had stilled itself; no breeze blew. Watching and waiting.

"It's quiet," I said softly.

"*Too* quiet," Skeet replied, grinning as he completed the cliché.

"Shut up, the both of you," Benjy muttered at us.

We took a gently sloping road along a row of narrow terraced houses. We saw nobody, even though it couldn't have been more than seven or eight o'clock. Fear of the Catchman had kept the kids and adults inside today, after the death of Rob Alder; but the Abbey Cross guys wouldn't be afraid, and they were almost always out and about at this hour. Still, we saw nothing of anyone. The soft thud of our footsteps seemed to get louder and louder, until it was beginning to get on my nerves.

I was hyped again, like I had been before. A cocktail of fear, excitement and adrenalin was making me jumpy, boosting my reactions. My eyes were feverishly alert, glimmering yellow in the dead light from the lamp-posts. A fat moon hung overhead.

Do they know we're coming? I thought.

No. They couldn't possibly. I'd only made my plan less than an hour ago, and nobody had had a chance to betray us even if they'd wanted too.

I vaguely considered the possibility that they were in mourning, or that the community was shocked at such a brutal stabbing. Two things wrong with that:

first, I didn't know if Jamie was dead or not. I've seen people take worse injuries than that and live through 'em. Second, there were usually one or two stabbings a year in this area anyway, so it was hardly likely to rock Abbey Cross to the core.

We went on anyway, unnerved by the silence.

That was pretty much when we walked into them.

Coming down a narrow path between two garden fences, we walked out into the small adventure playground area, with a couple of swings, a roundabout and a witch's hat. If I'd thought about it, I'd have realized that the roundabout was the same one that had alerted me by its squeaking the first time I came here. This time, we'd accidentally come upon it from a different angle.

Dumb. In that moment, the deserted streets were explained. The whole gang was gathered here, having a meeting, presumably to decide exactly how many hours of torture they were gonna put us through when they caught us.

To say we picked a bad time to arrive was an understatement.

The moment we came into view of the playground, we tried to back off, but luck wasn't with us. One of them had seen us emerge from the jitty, and that was it. We didn't stop to see what reaction his yell provoked among his mates; we just turned around and pegged it. Was this ever getting *repetitive*.

"Split up!" I cried, straight away. "Meet at the cross!"

Nobody needed to acknowledge my order; they all knew it was the best thing to do.

We'd barely come out of the other side of the jitty when Skeet grabbed Leanne by the wrist and pulled her with him, splitting off from us and racing the other way down the road. Benjy seemed about to protest, but right then a cacophony of shouts came from behind us, and he thought better of it.

We ripped down the road, skirting a head-high wall that held back a fringe of bare-limbed trees. The mob was practically baying for blood behind us. I was looping it, high on fear and excitement, and a manic grin was spread across my face. It was like I was riding on a crest of momentum so powerful that I couldn't stop running if I tried.

The road came up to a staggered junction, giving us three choices of where to go. I ran for the one going left, waving Benjy past me towards the one that led straight on. Bannon, predictably, followed him. Good. I was cut loose. Doing this kind of stuff on my own was always a lot more fun.

Once alone, I did my best to throw the pursuit. They weren't close behind me, but I knew they'd be fanning out across Abbey Cross right now; there were enough of them to give them a good chance of running into us. I jumped a hedge into someone's front garden. I'd got past the terraces now, into a road of detached properties – and tried their garden gate. Locked, like I thought.

Running footsteps, coming up the road that I'd just left. A lot of them. And I was way too visible.

I jumped up and grabbed the top of the gate. It juddered noisily under my weight – it was only a thin wooden thing – and the lock rattled. I hauled myself up and dragged myself over, disappearing just as the pursuit ran into the road. But the gate rattled again as I dropped down on the other side of it, going like a machine-gun in the still night.

"Over there!" one of them shouted.

I sprinted down the side of the house, racing past lighted windows. I saw one woman's look of surprise as I flashed by right in front of her, my dreads flapping behind me, our faces separated only by a pane of glass. I had just about reached the fence in the back garden by the time the Abbey Cross lads got over the gate. Another jump, a commando-roll over the top, and I realized that there wasn't another garden there at all; a narrow stream ran between the houses here, banked up with dried and hardened mud and reinforced with the roots of trees that grew alongside it.

I only had time for a moment of alarm before I landed, my ankle buckling on a root. I pitched forward, rolling down the bank and into the stream. The bruise on my ribs that Benjy had given me when we were threading Jamie Archer had been relatively quiet all day, but now it blazed up in pain. The shallow water splashed up all around me, soaking me instantly, but I was back up in a second, clambering up the other bank and running along it. I came out, flailing water, into a small cross-street, and dodged down an alley, past a cul-de-sac, and on to another road, and that was when I realized that the pursuit had disappeared. I'd lost them.

Allowing myself a breath of relief, I stopped to take stock. I was soaking wet, and pretty soon I'd be freezing cold as well. But I wasn't giving up because of a little thing like that. I had to get to the graveyard. That was where the answers were.

Although I was pretty much lost, it didn't take me long to reorientate myself. I hadn't strayed too far from where I wanted to go, so I found the road and got my bearings from there. Easy enough. I maintained a nonchalant pace, trying not to draw attention, as I walked over the road at a pelican crossing and then headed towards the cemetery.

I had decided long before I got there that trying to get in by either the main gate or the hole in the bars would be stupid; they were the most obvious places to get in, and surely some of the lads in Abbey Cross had figured out by now where we were going, and would be guarding them. Instead I approached via the grounds of an orphanage, which backed on to the high western wall of the cemetery.

Getting into the orphanage was easy, and though I set off a few security lights, nobody noticed me. I sneaked along the gravel path that ran around the back

162

of the huge, ramshackle property and into a car park. The surface under my feet turned to crunching rocks, chips of some kind of stone about the size of those fat marbles you used to be able to get.

I looked up briefly at the winter-stripped trees that grew against the wall, but their branches had been clipped back to prevent the orphans climbing them. I felt the surface of the wall, but there were no decent handholds for me to scale it, and the top lip was just too high for me to grab.

Oh well, I thought to myself. Guess it'll have to be the cars then.

Yeah, the staff of the orphanage had been careless enough to park their cars against the wall, providing a perfect springboard to jump off. I chose one which looked beat-up enough so it was unlikely to have an alarm – an old Vauxhall Cavalier. I leaned my weight on it, dipping it on its suspension, just to be sure, and then hopped up on its bonnet.

The metal dented with a loud crack like the sound of a lift cable snapping. I ignored it, stepping on to the roof, which was just as unhappy about having to bear the full weight of someone like me. It just wasn't designed to take that kind of stress, and it buckled in a little like the bonnet.

Cosmetic damage, I assured myself. Won't cost them much to fix. And then I jumped up, grabbed the top of the wall, and pulled myself up on top of it.

I suppose if I said it was deathly quiet it'd sort of be

in bad taste, wouldn't it? Okay, let's just say it was silent, the way cemeteries at night always are. Out of the light from the street, the moon had taken over, spreading everything with its blue and silver glow. The sea of gravestones lapped beneath my feet, and from my position high on the wall I could see the old tomb with the big Saxon cross, guarded by spider-limbed trees.

After a few moments of looking around, checking to see if anybody was in the graveyard with me, I slid down from the wall and dropped quietly to the turf with a soft thud. I was still very aware that there could be Abbey Cross guys around in here, not to mention something much, much worse.

I hoped Skeet and Leanne were okay. As for Benjy and Bannon . . . well, if they were caught, at least they'd fulfil a useful role as punchbags while the rest of us got away.

But first, the tomb. I had my own private agenda, and it had nothing to do with meeting the Catchman, no matter what I'd said to Benjy. I wasn't *that* stupid.

18

I dodged among the gravestones, keeping low, stopping every few graves to listen. Nothing. I think I hated the silence more than anything. I kept on glancing over my shoulder; I couldn't help myself. It was just that I expected any second to feel those cold hands around my neck, the fingers crossing over my windpipe, throttling the life out of me...

I began to shiver. My cold, damp clothes and hair were finally beginning to get to me. At least it was a warmish night and there was no wind like there was last time, but even so, I knew I'd come out of this with at least a cold, if not pneumonia. Still, if that was the worst thing that happened tonight, I'd count myself lucky.

Nothing rose up to challenge me as I made my way closer to the tomb. I saw no other sign of life in the graveyard. Sometimes distant shouts came to me, the Abbey Cross lads calling angrily to each other. I cherished the break in the silence but I didn't pay any attention to them. They weren't my problem right now.

So here it was. The tomb. Course, if I'd just wanted to hang out at the Abbey Cross tomb, I could have come along on my own. But that wasn't my reason for being here. Nor was I gonna have it out with the

Catchman. That was just a ruse to get Benjy to come. The Catchman was a problem that could be easily solved; after all, he'd only ever haunted this city. All I had to do was leave, like Skeet had been bugging me to do.

But I needed everyone along, so I could make my escape with Skeet and Leanne. See, Leanne would only come with Benjy, and tonight I planned to get her. Steal her from right under Benjy's nose.

Skeet had known exactly what he was doing when he ran off with her. Separating her from Benjy, just like we'd arranged. And then we were gonna meet up here.

I hid just by the path that circled the tomb. I looked around, peering into shadows until I was sure there was nobody about. My arms were beginning to ache with the cold and the amount of climbing I'd been doing recently, but the anticipation of what I was gonna pull off here made it all worthwhile. Crouching behind a gravestone, I settled to wait for Skeet, with his precious cargo in tow.

My eyes wandered to the inscription on the gravestone in front of me, and I was trying to read it without the benefit of my torch (which I didn't dare use) when I heard a sound. It was a sound I'd heard once before, but never when I was awake: the sound of a dog whining, but not just *any* dog – *the* dog. The one my dad had been skinning in my dream.

"Dad?" I said, not daring to look round.

"*Here, son,*" came his voice from behind me.

"Are *you* the Catchman?"

There was a low chuckle. "*No, Davey, I'm just a creation of your mind, a hallucination. Your head never did work quite properly, did it? Especially not after you found me and your mum that day. You've always known it, haven't you?*"

"The things I saw. . ." I said quietly. "The writing in the book . . . the car park . . . nobody could have done those things. Nobody could have faked them."

"*You could, Davey,*" came the reply. "*Don't you remember? I used to be so good at it. And you've learned a lot from your old dad.*"

The dog whined anew in the background.

"No," I said, beginning to tremble. "I'm *not* crazy. You're *not* there."

"*So turn around and look, Davey.*"

I didn't want to. I was terrified of what I might see there. I stayed, with my eyes fixed on the gravestone.

"*Don't you want to know the truth, Davey?*" came the voice again, mocking me.

"Not from you," I said, my voice slow and measured. "You're not real. I'm not playing along with a delusion."

"*That's right, I am a delusion,*" came the reply. "*Just like in the car park. Just like when you heard that poor girl speak to you in the Catchman's voice. Just like a lot of things, Davey.*"

I was silent, my teeth digging into my lower lip, my

eyes squeezed shut. Time seemed to stretch out, prolonging the nightmare. He *wasn't* there, *wasn't*.

That was when I noticed the dog had stop whining. And the voice, the voice of my dad, had departed. I let out a shuddering sigh. Was he right? *Was* it all in my head? Would I end up like him, swiping at phantoms of my own imagination? Or could I keep it all under control? The questions lapped up inside me like waves, threatening to swamp me, foaming panic as they broke. But panic was one thing I couldn't do right now, because there was still a terrible danger out there. I hadn't lied when I said that I thought the Catchman was watching us, and that he wouldn't be able to resist if we came to the cemetery. I'd guarantee that he'd know what we were up to tonight.

That was when I realized that the shouts I'd heard before had moved a lot closer while I was crouching here, dumbstruck. The mob had obviously worked out where we'd gone, and was following us into the cemetery. I hunkered down into the underbrush of gravestones a moment before a bunch of guys emerged from another direction.

"There was one of 'em here," he said. "I'm sure I saw 'im."

I stayed crouched behind the tall gravestone, watching and listening to them argue it out, cursing under my breath. This was where I was supposed to meet up with Skeet and Leanne. How was I gonna do that now, with these guys here? I knew that if I waited for them to turn up, we could probably peg it before these guys knew what was going on, but. . .

No, I had to find them, intercept them. We couldn't afford to be caught by Abbey Cross now. I turned and silently crept away through the gravestones, listening to the voices fading behind me. My eyes scanned the dark cemetery while my brain burned feverishly, trying to figure out where they'd be. I tried to put myself in Skeet's place; nobody knew him better than me. Where would he go? How would he come into the cemetery, if he wasn't here already?

There it was; the answer. *How would he come into the cemetery?* Skeet was nothing if not predictable. He'd go for the most obvious way, because he wouldn't be bothered to think of alternatives. And he'd never been here before; he didn't know about the back way, and had only a vague idea of where the cemetery was. He'd come to it off a main road; that meant the front gate.

I was so inspired by my deduction, so distracted, that it took a few seconds before my brain cottoned on to what my eyes were seeing in the distance.

Over the wall of the cemetery, the same place where I had crossed, a black and hooded figure slipped across my vision, flowing like ink. Coming in. The Catchman.

I stopped breathing for a moment. He was here. Almost unconsciously, my butterfly knife came out of my pocket, snickering open. He wasn't gonna catch me unprepared this time.

I tried to keep my eyes on him, but as soon as he hit the ground he was gone, using the gravestones for cover in the same way that I did. I began to move, heading slowly towards the main gate but keeping my eyes on where the Catchman had been, searching for another glimpse. My throat had gone dry, and swallowing was kinda painful. Staying crouched for too long had set off my shivers again. But I ignored the discomfort, weaving between the stones, hurrying low to the ground, heading for where I hoped I'd find Leanne and Skeet.

I had nearly reached the tall, iron bars of the gate, flanked by angelic sentries, when I caught a sensation of movement out of the corner of my eye. I stopped, peering at the spot where I thought I'd seen it. Nothing. I looked around nervously, hemmed in by the gravestones on all sides.

There – it came again. Twin eyes shone at me from the darkness. A cat or something. I swore at it under my breath.

And then a pair of cold, leathery hands slipped around my throat from behind.

I thrashed, filled with revulsion and fear at the touch, but a weight fell on my back, bearing me down and pinning my knife under me. My face was pushed into the turf, and the fingers on my neck interlaced and fastened tight.

I tried to hitch in a breath, but no air would fill the vacuum in my chest. Panicking, I wormed an arm free,

170

digging backwards with my elbow, hoping to hit my attacker in the chest; but I hit nothing once again. Stars were beginning to dance in front of my eyes, and a roaring, dazzling sea of sparks was steadily encroaching on my vision, coming in from the edges. Lack of oxygen, I thought faintly. I struggled, but the fight was impossible, and gradually my struggles weakened and the blackness overwhelmed me.

19

"... yoky?"

"... keet ... watiff ... ed?"

"... vey?"

"*Davey!*"

My body spasmed, as if I'd just woken from dream of falling a second before I hit the ground and then my eyes flew open. Skeet was leaning over me. Instinctively, I scrambled backwards along the ground, thinking he was the Catchman, animal fear in my eyes.

Why hadn't he killed me?

"Davey! Davey, it's alright," another voice came, this one unbearably sweet to my ears at that moment. And then Leanne was kneeling by me, her hands on my arm and my shoulder, soothing me.

My face broke into a grin of utter relief as I saw her. I was alive.

"Have..." I said, then coughed and tried again through my aching throat. "Are you two alright?"

They looked at each other quizzically. "Yeah. Course," Leanne said.

I let my head fall back. "Benjy," I rasped. "It was Benjy."

There was no reply from either of them, just a stunned silence.

"Benjy," I said. "He got me. You must've interrupted him."

"We heard somethin'," Skeet said, "but we just found you like this. She nearly tripped over you, you mook." He paused. "We scared him off, I guess."

"Hey, whoa, *wait* a minute!" Leanne hissed. "How can you—"

"I *saw* him, okay?" I snapped, massaging my aching neck. "And I've felt those hands on my throat before. He's the Catchman!"

Leanne was gaping, horror in her eyes. "I always thought. . ." she said brokenly. "But I didn't believe . . . he can't be."

"He is," I said, choking. "He is, and if you go back to him, he'll know you know."

"Help him up," said Skeet to Leanne. He got his arm under me, and Leanne followed suit. Together they helped me to my knees. Skeet sighed. "Let's get outta here. There ain't no reason to stay any more."

"What about Benjy?" Leanne asked, desperately, looking from Skeet to me. "Won't he—"

"You go with Skeet," I interrupted. "Don't worry about Benjy." I picked up my knife where it had been squashed into the turf. "I'll find him."

"Davey, don't. Don't hurt him please!" she cried.

"I don't know what I'm gonna do," I said.

Skeet looked at me levelly, trying to work out what I was doing, and then blinked in resignation. He knew

173

me well enough. I wouldn't be persuaded to come until I'd done what I had to do.

Leanne's eyes were regarding me tearfully. "We can just ... we can leave him behind. So he's the Catchman, so what? You don't need to face him. We can just go!" she said.

"I'll meet you two outside the arcade," I said.

"Alright," Skeet said, and his gormless face held an expression that said: *I hope you know what you're doing.* Then he turned to Leanne. "C'mon, let's go."

She gave me one last, reluctant look, and then went with him. I think it had all happened too fast for her to really gather what was going on. In her eyes, this was the final proof; but it was a terrible wrench for her. Together, they ran back towards the gate.

I gave them a minute or so to get gone and decided to start back for the tomb. That was as good a place as any to begin searching. I was angry now, really angry.

But my anger wasn't for the Catchman. He was an impossible enemy. I couldn't fight him; I knew that now. It would be like trying to wrestle a ghost, a phantom composed of the myths and legends of the city. All I could do was avoid him long enough to do what I had to do and then get away. Besides, he'd unwittingly done me a favour. Leanne couldn't help but believe me now.

This wasn't finished yet, and I couldn't leave until it was. I had to get Benjy out of the picture, one way or another. It was the only way I could keep Leanne.

I'd convinced her that Benjy was the Catchman, even though he wasn't. That had been the last part of the plan. But now I realized that I had to end it, here and now. Because I could never rest easy if I knew he was out there, looking for me – for *us*.

But you know it's not Benjy that's doing all this, a voice inside me said.

I didn't care. I was gonna kill him anyway.

Gripping my knife tight, I lurched through the cemetery, not caring about the Abbey Cross lot any more (though they seemed to have mainly given up and gone home) but thinking only of the Catchman. This was gonna be the final showdown.

My teeth gritted hard, I went through the still, moonlit night, looking from gravestone to gravestone, treading over the silver-grassed turf. The pain of being strangled couldn't stop me now. I'd had enough. It was time to finish this, and finish it for good.

Then to my right, I heard a noise; a word, spoken. I couldn't make out what was said, but I went for it anyway, homing in on the sound. A strip of moonlight limned my blade. It had to be him. Creeping quietly, I stole up on where I thought the sound had come from.

I saw two things: Bannon, dead on the ground, his eyes wide and staring, and Benjy, leaning over him.

And then I screamed out a cry of hate, and went for him.

20

I shouldn't have warned him with that cry, but I couldn't help myself. All the frustration, all the wasted time and pointless aggravation and swagger and everything I hated about him came boiling up and out of my throat. All the things he'd done to Leanne, even the way she stubbornly clung to him. He was gonna pay for all of that.

But though he was a big guy, he was fast. Turning, he saw me lunging towards him, and instinctively he reacted. He grabbed my wrist and threw me, doing one of those judo moves he was so good at. I went flying on to the soft turf, my leg exploding in agony, but I rolled and I was back on my feet in seconds, my knife held out before me.

"*This* time we sort it *all* out," I breathed, sparing a glance down at Bannon.

Benjy's face twisted into a snarl, and a knife appeared in his hands, pulled from Bannon's dead fingers. "I've been waiting to deal with you for a long time," he said.

"And the winner gets Leanne," I said, a tight smile on my face.

"You ain't gonna win," he replied, and he lunged at me.

I dodged out of his way, avoiding the knife and

hammering a left-handed punch home into his stomach. It didn't faze him; he whipped out his own left hand and caught me a backfist across the face. I staggered away from him, testing the bruise with the back of my knife hand.

"You always thought you were good," he sneered at me. "Time to see, know what I mean?"

I didn't bother with a reply to that; I just dived in, slashing at his face. Somehow, his own blade whipped up and parried with a sharp, punching ring, but I'd overextended myself, too eager, and I stumbled forward. He planted an elbow in the side of my back and tripped me at the same time. I had a fast impression of a gravestone rushing towards me before I hit it, my head glancing off the stone, but the pain didn't strike me till I'd regained my feet again. The spot where I'd hit it was a blaze of agony and it felt wet, but when I put my fingers there, there was no blood.

"Careful," Benjy said sarcastically. "Don't hurt yourself."

I cried out in rage and ran for him, my hair a whipping nest of snakes; but at the last moment, I stopped, throwing my blade to my other hand, and lashed out at him. Wrongfooted, he didn't move quickly enough, and the edge scored along the back of his knife hand. He swore loudly, dropping the knife, but managed to rabbit-punch me in the stomach with his other hand and I went back, gasping for breath.

Then he leaped at me, knowing that he didn't have

a chance with his knife hand out of action unless mine was too. He bundled me to the ground, pinning me, and grabbed my right wrist, smashing my knuckles against a gravestone until they ran with blood, and eventually I had to let go with a yell. At the same time I wormed my arm free and tried to push him off, but his weight was too much. He began pounding me with blows, raining them down on my face and chest, and I was trying to fight back but I didn't have any leverage. He was trying to pummel me to death; I saw the same look on his face he'd had when he was kicking Jamie Archer.

Then, somehow, my thrashings managed to free my shoulders. "Get *off* me," I cried, and headbutted him square in the nose. It did the job. He clambered away, shoving himself back off me with his hands.

I stood up, my chest heaving, face dirt-smeared and bloodied, looking like a wild animal as I faced him. I glanced around, and my eyes fell on the silver sheen of my knife blade in the grass where it had fallen. Benjy saw it too, and dived for it at the same moment as I did. We crashed together, scrabbling frantically for a moment before breaking apart and coming to our feet. When we did, it was my hand that was holding the blade.

Benjy flexed his hands, looking at the knife that I held. He was sizing up his chances of taking me when I had a weapon and he didn't. His muscles bunched, ready to spring . . . then he turned and ran.

I was so surprised that, for a moment, I didn't follow him. My surprise didn't last long. Cheated of my satisfaction, I yelled "Hey!" after him, and then broke into a sprint.

My lips skinned back from my teeth, my eyes blazing, I went after him. There was no way Benjy was getting away from me this time. The gravestones blurred past me on either side, barely seen. My gaze was locked on him, scrambling away from me, dodging clumsily through the maze of epitaphs, panicking.

Like I told you before, I can be fast when I want and I was hyped off my box now. I'd feel the pain of my battered body later. Right now, I was just a bundle of anger, and I wasn't half done with Benjy yet.

He looked back at me, his face a picture of fear, and redoubled his efforts, running towards the iron fence with the gap in the railings that would allow him freedom. No good. I'd catch him way before that, and he knew it.

I closed the distance fast, my teeth gritted and my dreads whipping about as I hunted him through the labyrinth of waist-high gravestones. I was almost on top of him when he hit a clear patch, a small, empty lot where there was only smooth grass. I pounced, rugby-tackling him in the back, and his forward momentum sent him toppling on to the turf. He tried to scrabble away, turning over and crabwalking backwards, but I jumped on him and pressed the edge of the knife to his throat, and he stopped still.

"It wasn't me!" he cried. "Bannon was dead when I found him! It was someone else who did it! *Someone else!*"

For a long minute our eyes were locked, one in terror, the other in hatred.

"Davey," he said, his voice pleading. "Remember what I said? About the myth? You're letting it get to you, Davey. There's a killer out there, but it's not me!"

I blinked. "*I* know that," I said. "It's *me*."

Then I threw the knife aside and clamped my hands around his neck. He tried to thrash, but it didn't do any good. My hands were crushing his throat, my thumbs crossing over his windpipe and pressing in . . . and I squeezed.

My knees had his forearms pinned; he couldn't move, couldn't do anything but stare and wonder how it could all have come to this. His chest spasmed between my legs, trying to pull in a breath that wasn't there. His tongue bulged out of his mouth. His eyes were wide, so wide that I could see the fine blood vessels in the moonlight.

And then he went limp, with a last horrible gargling noise, and the light in his eyes died.

I released his throat, and the smell of foul air seeped out between his teeth in a long sigh. Tidal breath. They all did that. The last ten per cent or so of the lungs was never emptied unless you fainted or died.

I sat back on his belly, and looked up at the sky. Strangely, it had cleared overhead, and the stars shone through brightly. A breeze had sprung up at last, stirring the still night, rattling the bony trees.

You lose, I thought looking down at Benjy. *I win.*

The lads from Abbey Cross had probably just given up the chase and gone home, but to me it seemed like reverence. They knew the game was finished, and they didn't want to fight any more. Whatever the reason, though, my way was clear as I walked out of the cemetery. Nobody appeared to hassle me. I didn't see a single person. There was only quiet, and the steadily approaching iron railings that would let me out of this place for good.

You killed him, I thought to myself. *Dad was right. You're a murderer, just like he is. You are him. Like father, like son.*

I sighed, the terrible ache in my neck and body settling in. I was too wasted to think about it now. All I wanted to do was stumble to where I was meeting Skeet and Leanne, and after that. . .

. . .after that, what? After that, we were gone. That was it – just leaving. Me, Skeet and Leanne. None of us had any ties here any more. Find a new city and disappear into it, just like we'd done with this one. The cops would never find us; we operate below their level. We were only witnesses to Jamie's stabbing; it had been Benjy that had actually *done* it. We were nothing to them. Benjy's death would be put down to the Catchman, and that suited me fine.

I didn't think I'd tell Leanne about what I'd done to Benjy. It might mess with my chances with her. I'd tell her I never found him, just Bannon's body. Maybe one day she'd read about him in the papers and think he was strangled by the Catchman. Whatever. That was something that was beyond my control.

Anyway, enough. I reached the railings, a terrible exhaustion setting in from my ordeal. Past them, the narrow streets of Abbey Cross brooded, dark and uncaring. I put my hand on one of the bent railings, angling my shoulder to slip through –

– and I heard a footstep behind me, a heavy crunch of twigs.

Not now. I thought. *I'm too tired to—*

But by then I had turned, and my thoughts plunged into the black pit that seemed to open in the base of my brain. My legs weakened and I fell back against the railings; it was only them that stopped me falling to the ground.

Standing before me, less than three metres away, was the Catchman. The tall, lean figure stood silently, draped in his black habit. The blank, heavy darkness of the hood looked back at me.

Three words were circling in my head, end to end to end: *it's not fair it's not fair it's not fair*. My strength deserted me. I knew I couldn't fight him now, not after all I'd been through. Like a vulture he had waited

182

until I had exhausted myself, patiently watching from a distance ... and now that I was helpless, he had shown his hand at last.

I just hung there, slumped against the railing, mutely waiting for whatever he had in store for me.

For a long time, there was no movement from him, the figure that had been trying to kill me ever since I had first seen him in the graveyard. Why? Because I was the only one who had seen him and lived? Maybe. Maybe I'd never know. Just like I'd never know why he killed ... only that I'd led him to Mos Eisley, which was like leading a cat into a cage full of mice.

He just stood there, watching me, penetrating me with his invisible stare.

Then slowly, *slowly*, he nodded his hooded head. A nod of acknowledgement. A nod of respect, as to an equal or to a kindred spirit. And then he turned and walked away, and the shadows welled up to greet him, and he was gone.

I stood there, dumbstruck. Then I began to laugh. First quietly, then the spasmodic chuckles took hold, and finally I was laughing uncontrollably, stripping my throat raw, my chest aching as I verged on hysteria.

He's a fruitloop, Benjy's voice spoke up in my head, echoing the past. *Guess it runs in the family*.

You are me, came Dad's voice one more time, and this time it was assured of its own rightness.

Yeah, I thought. *I am you and I am him and he is us. We're all the same, we fruitloops. You, me, the*

Catchman. . . The only thing you messed up, Dad, is that you offed yourself as well as Mum. The rest of us, though . . . we came out of it okay.

We came out of it okay? Yeah, I guess we did, I told myself, still laughing. This changed nothing. Benjy was still the Catchman – at least, that's what I'd be telling Leanne. By the time she found different, she'd be well away with me. I'd done what I wanted to. Benjy was gone and I had Leanne. All ties were cut. Re*sult*.

I staggered out of the cemetery and through the streets, my laughter reverberating through the breezy night air, chasing its own echoes down the streets of Abbey Cross. The future was open now; me, Skeet and Leanne were ready to start a new life together. There were cities upon cities out there for us to lose ourselves in, and I was gonna go to them.

I didn't have anything better to do.

About the Author

Chris Wooding was born in Leicester in 1977 and his first book was published when he was just nineteen years old. He studied English Literature at Sheffield University and now lives in London. He has written several books, including the *Broken Sky* series, *Crashing, Kerosene, Catchman* and most recently the acclaimed novels *The Haunting of Alaizabel Cray* and *Poison*.

POISON

IT **WAS** Snapdragon's scream that jerked Poison awake.
She half-rose out of her blankets, sloughing off a thin
dusting of sparkling flakes that covered her. Strangely,
despite the circumstances of her waking, she immediately
felt the warm hand of sleep enfolding her again, making her
eyes droop. She shook herself in puzzlement, looking down
at the stuff on her blanket and in her hair. It was like
unmelted snow, yet it glimmered in the cloudy light of the
morning sun that came in through the round window.

She felt herself drowsing again, against her will, and this
time she flung her blankets aside and pulled herself out of
the tattered old bed. The flakes . . . it was something to do
with the flakes. . . She did not understand how or why, but
some instinct had made the connection between the
mysterious stuff that covered the bed and the weight of
slumber that pressed down on her. She tousled and shook
her hair and patted down her hemp nightrobe frantically, as
if trying to beat out flames, and she felt her tiredness lift
from her as the flakes fell free. She stared at them in

alarmed wonder for a moment.

"What have you *done?*" Snapdragon shrieked at her from the other side of the small room, and Poison suddenly remembered why it was she had been awoken. Snapdragon was standing at Azalea's cradle, her face a rictus of horror, her eyes needling accusation at Poison.

Poison rubbed a hand across her face to smear the last remnants of sleep from her eyes and came over to the crib, ignoring Snapdragon completely. There was a terrible sinking in her chest, a spreading void of premonition.

She looked into the crib. Whatever it was that lay in there, it was not Azalea.

"Why didn't you wake?" Snapdragon hissed. "You were right there! You terrible thing! Why didn't you wake?"

Poison was not listening. The world seemed to have shrunk to the size of the crib, and what was inside it. Sounds had become faint, even Snapdragon's shrill voice in her ear. She could hear the slow whoosh of blood as it swept round her body, the inrush and release of her breath. She put her hands on the side of the crib to steady herself. Somewhere in her memory, a small silver bell was chiming.

She pushed herself away from the crib and snatched down the thickest tome on her bookshelf. She had borrowed it from Fleet a long time ago, and never thought to give it back. Its dusty leather cover creaked as she opened it, and the pages flickered under her fingers.

"Reading? Reading at a time like this?" Snapdragon howled. Poison spared her an annoyed glance before resuming her search. Her stepmother began to weep. "Poor

Hew. What'll I tell him? What'll I say? His heart will break."

The page that Poison was looking for flipped flat, and she felt her head go light. There it was. The leftmost page was dominated by a black-and-white woodcut print of a hunched figure dressed in a long, ragged coat, its face shadowed under a wide-brimmed hat. Its eyes were two slits in the darkness. It held out before it one long, thin arm, and its scrawny, emaciated hand held a tiny bell delicately between thumb and forefinger. With its other hand, it was scattering something that looked like dust. In the picture, it was in a wooded glade, surrounded by sleeping people.

"The Scarecrow," she whispered.

Poison heard the chime again in her head. She frowned, puzzled, and stared hard at the page. Had she seen something *move* there, just a moment ago? She peered closer.

The picture suddenly seemed to grow under her gaze, as if she was falling into it or it was rising from the page to swallow her. The black-and-white leaves of the trees seemed to stir. She felt dizzy, her violet eyes going wide.

The Scarecrow turned its head to look at her, staring out from the page, and her throat tightened in terror. She wanted to close the book suddenly, but she could not will her muscles to move. She felt herself pinned there, unable to even blink. Disbelief and panic clawed their way upward from her chest.

The Scarecrow began to walk towards her. Its movements were curiously jerky, as if she was watching a flicker-book, but it was definitely moving. Coming closer in short, hobbling steps, its tiny bell held out before it.

Impossible, she told herself. *Impossible*.

But she could not draw back, could not look away. The chime sounded again as the Scarecrow twitched the bell, a pure and unutterably sinister note, quiet and yet clearer than anything else she could hear. It had loomed until its upper body almost filled the page now, as if she was looking at it through a window and it was almost at the sill. The bell chimed again, dominating her consciousness. The white slits of the Scarecrow's eyes burned into her from within the inky darkness of its face.

Poison could barely breathe. What air she could force into her lungs came in shudders. Everything she knew was telling her that this could not be happening, that it was only a picture on a page she was looking at; and yet the Scarecrow grew, shuffling closer and closer until it seemed that there was only the thickness of the page separating them.

It put one hand on the edge of the picture, and its fingers folded over the bottom of the page and scraped against her wrist.

The slam of the outside door jolted her out of her trance, and she flung the book away with a cry. It tumbled to the floor and landed shut with a heavy thump on the planks. Trembling, she stared at it from her bed, ready to run if it should do anything other than lie where it was.

Nothing happened.

Poison felt her heartbeat decelerate slowly, and began to breathe again. She clasped her hands in her lap to try and stop them shaking, stealing glances at the book now and again. There must be an explanation, there must be. . .

It was then that she noticed that Snapdragon was gone, and married that realization to the slam of the hut door she had heard a moment ago. The crib was empty too.

In a flash, she saw what Snapdragon was going to do; and she scrambled off her bed and fled out of the door to try and stop her.

∽∾∽

It was a cold and dank morning, the sun clambering up through the faintly greenish miasma that hung over the Black Marshes. A little early still for the flies to be out, for the waters of the marsh had not yet warmed to the day's heat. Poison emerged from her hut into the chill, clad only in her hemp nightdress. It did not bother her overly: most of the village was still abed after the excitement of Soulswatch Eve, and though she looked faintly ridiculous, her nightdress was thicker and warmer than her daywear and she did not care what the villagers thought anyway. She had the sense to pause to put on some boots though, for it was virtually suicide to walk barefoot in the mud of the marsh, where there were insects and snakes, venomous spiders and spiny snails underfoot, any of which could kill with a bite or a scratch.

Snapdragon was nowhere to be seen, but there was only one bridge from their platform to the next, so she hurried over it to her neighbour's platform, where the wraith-catcher snored in Bluff's house while Bluff and his wife made do with the floor. Two rope bridges branched off from there; one of them was still swinging slightly in the wake of Snapdragon's passage. Poison took it, already knowing where Snapdragon was going.

She caught sight of her stepmother just as she was disappearing into the trees that crowded up against the lake in which Gull stood. The thing that had been in the crib was wrapped up tight in a blanket, held against her chest. Poison called out to her as she ran on to the rope-bridge that spanned the murky water from shore to village. Snapdragon paused momentarily and looked back, and there was a kind of madness in her expression; then she plunged on into the trees. Poison rushed after her and slipped on the moist planking of the bridge, but she caught the ropes at either side with her armpits before she could fall, and she suffered only sore burns on her skin. Cursing herself, she ran on and into the marsh.

The ground squelched beneath her boots as she followed Snapdragon. This was relatively solid ground as far as the Black Marshes went, and she knew it to be mercifully free of bogs and sinkholes. She caught a glimpse of her stepmother's blonde braid swinging ahead of her through the trees. Something crunched under her boot, but she did not stop to see what unfortunate creature she had stepped on. The trees had been chopped back a little way here, forming a bumpy trail that had been flattened down by innumerable feet. She put on speed and began catching up with Snapdragon, who was slowing as she ran out of breath, until by the time they got to the well Poison was almost close enough to touch her.

The well sat in the middle of a roughly hewn clearing, a

stone-lined shaft with square walls that rose out of the ground to waist-height. A tight, rusty grille lay over the shaft, and a roof above that. The roof was sloped inward to a funnel, so that any rainwater it caught was spouted down into the shaft. Rainwater was fine, and so was the clear water from the underground spring that the well fed off; but they did not want any of the murky surface pollution of the marsh to get into their precious drinking supply, nor any slimy marsh creatures to fall in, hence the wall and the grille.

Snapdragon stumbled to her knees as she entered the clearing, dropping her burden to the soft earth. It made not a sound. When Poison reached her, she was hyper-ventilating great whoops of air.

"Here, here, do this," Poison said, her impatient tone masking real concern. She pulled Snapdragon's sleeve over her hand and put it to her stepmother's mouth. "Hold that."

Snapdragon did so with her free hand while Poison pulled the sleeve tight at her elbow, cutting off the air and making a reasonable cloth bag for Snapdragon to breathe into. She gasped a little more, but soon she was breathing normally again, and finally Poison let her go.

"You shouldn't get so excited," Poison advised.

Snapdragon sagged, her eyes falling to the bundle on the ground before her. "It's so heavy," she said.

Poison looked at where it lay, eerily still. She had wrapped it up like a loaf of bread. She wondered whether it was breathing or not. Then she wondered if it needed to.

"You were going to put it in the well?" she asked.

"I can't let Hew see it! It would kill him!"

"Don't be an idiot!" Poison snapped back. "For one thing, you'd pollute the water supply if you left it rotting down there; hadn't you thought of that? Besides, you can't drown it. Don't you know what that thing is?"

Snapdragon gave her a furious glare. She hated being made to feel ignorant. "I suppose *you* do?"

"It's a changeling," Poison said. "A changeling. And if you'd put it down that well, we'd never get Azalea back."

Snapdragon looked at her in disbelief. "How do you know? How do you *know*, you little witch? Did you do it to her? Did you?"

Poison did not bother to answer that. Instead, she scooped up the bundle – and it *was* heavy, like carrying stone rather than flesh – and looked down on where Snapdragon had begun to sob in the mud, her dress slimed and ruined.

"Say nothing of this. I will deal with it."

"Where has Azalea gone? What are you going to do?" Snapdragon called after her as she walked away.

"Say nothing of this," Poison called back, partly because she wanted Snapdragon to understand how important that was, partly because she did not know the answer to either of her questions.

But one man would.

CRASHING

Chris Wooding

So here it was – the party to mark the beginning of the summer. I guess we'd all brought our own agendas; mine was to get it together with Jo Anderson.

But everyone knows stuff like that never goes to plan. Friends were rapidly turning into enemies. The local mob of street-thug wannabes had declared virtual war on me. And looming over it all was the spectre of the Zone, the derelict estate haunted by stoners, psychos and freaks, calling me back one last time. Now I just needed to get my friends on board…

KEROSENE

Chris Wooding

Cal's got this thing about fire. It's nothing
big at first, just lighting matches, watching them
burn, enjoying the calming effects of the flame…
It helps him cope with stuff.

Then he meets Abby, and things start
to get out of control. She winds him up, playing
with him until he thinks he might lose his sanity, and
suddenly the matches just aren't enough any more.
So a plan hatches itself in Cal's mind, a plan so glorious it could set the world alight.
Nothing will ever touch him again…

ENDGAME

Chris Wooding

Humankind stands on the brink of
another war. A countdown has begun that could
bring about the end of the world…

Four friends must come to terms with the
impending conflict. But in the week up to zero hour,
friendships fail and new ones are forged as everyone
is forced to decide who and what
is really precious to them.

As a city erupts in violence and another
deadly threat emerges, old scores are settled that have
lain festering for years. But when the clock finishes
ticking, will there be war, or a last-minute retreat?
And which of the friends and friendships will
emerge unscathed from the chaos?

THE
HAUNTING
OF
ALAIZABEL CRAY

Chris Wooding

**Amongst the dark streets of London
dwells unimaginable terror…**

It happened after the Vernichtung – the war
left the city damaged, bruised, battered, its people
shattered and battle-scarred, and open
to a terrifying retribution…

Foul things lurk within the labyrinth of the Old
Quarter, and those who venture out at night are easy
prey. Prey for the wolves and murderers that stalk
the crooked streets, and for creatures far
more deadly – the wych-kin.

But evil disguised is deadliest of all.
And behind the façade of wealth and charity that
surrounds the uppermost levels of society lies
a terrifying pact with the wych-kin that
threatens humankind's very existence.

At its heart is the beautiful, vulnerable,
enigmatic Alaizabel Cray – key to the ultimate evil.